The Wedding in White

Also by Diana Palmer
in Large Print:

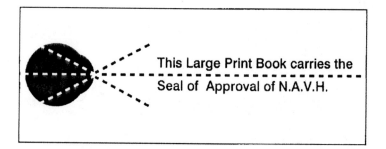

This Large Print Book carries the
Seal of Approval of N.A.V.H.

The Wedding in White

Diana Palmer

Published in 2006 by arrangement with Harlequin Books S.A.

Wheeler Large Print Romance.

The text of this Large Print edition is unabridged.
Other aspects of the book may vary from the original edition.

Set in 16 pt. Plantin by Ramona Watson.

Printed in the United States on permanent paper.

Library of Congress Cataloging-in-Publication Data

Palmer, Diana.
    The wedding in white / by Diana Palmer.
      p. cm. — (Wheeler Publishing large print romance)
    ISBN 1-59722-234-8 (lg. print : hc : alk. paper)
    1. Women teachers — Fiction. 2. Cattle breeders —
Fiction. 3. Texas — Fiction. I. Title. II. Wheeler large
print romance series.
PS3566.A513W43 2006
  813´.54—dc22   2006005922

The Wedding in White

As the Founder/CEO of NAVH, the only national health agency solely devoted to those who, although not totally blind, have an eye disease which could lead to serious visual impairment, I am pleased to recognize Thorndike Press* as one of the leading publishers in the large print field.

Founded in 1954 in San Francisco to prepare large print textbooks for partially seeing children, NAVH became the pioneer and standard setting agency in the preparation of large type.

Today, those publishers who meet our standards carry the prestigious "Seal of Approval" indicating high quality large print. We are delighted that Thorndike Press is one of the publishers whose titles meet these standards. We are also pleased to recognize the significant contribution Thorndike Press is making in this important and growing field.

Lorraine H. Marchi, L.H.D.
Founder/CEO
NAVH

* Thorndike Press encompasses the following imprints: Thorndike, Wheeler, Walker and Large Print Press.

Chapter 1

"I'll never get married!" Vivian wailed. "He won't let me have Whit here at all. I only wanted him to come for supper, and now I have to call him and say it's off! Mack's just hateful!"

"There, there," Natalie Brock soothed, hugging the younger girl. "He's not hateful. He just doesn't understand how you feel about Whit. And you have to remember, he's been totally responsible for you since you were fifteen."

"But he's my brother, not my father," came the sniffling reply. Vivian dashed tears off on the back of her hand. "I'm twenty-two," she added in a plaintive tone. "He can't tell me what to do anymore, anyway!"

"He can, on Medicine Ridge Ranch," Natalie reminded her wryly. Medicine Ridge Ranch was the largest spread in this part of Montana — even the town was named after it. "He's the big boss."

"Hmmph!" Vivian dabbed at her red eyes with a handkerchief. "Only because Daddy left it to him."

"That isn't quite true," came the amused rejoinder. "Your father left him a ranch that was almost bankrupt, on land the bank was trying to repossess." She waved her hand around the expensive Victorian furnishings of the living room. "All this came from his hard work, not a will."

"And so whatever McKinzey Donald Killain wants, he gets," Vivian raged.

It was odd to hear him called by his complete name. For years, everyone around Medicine Ridge, Montana, which had grown up around the Killain ranch, had called him Mack. It was an abbreviation of his first name, which few of his childhood friends could pronounce.

"He only wants you to be happy," Natalie said softly, kissing the flushed cheek of the blond girl. "I'll go talk to him."

"Would you?" Bright blue eyes looked up hopefully.

"I will."

"You're just the nicest friend anybody ever had, Nat," Vivian said fervently. "Nobody else around here has the guts to say anything to him," she added.

"Bob and Charles don't feel comfortable telling him what to do." Natalie defended the younger brothers of the household.

Mack had been responsible for all three of his siblings from his early twenties. He was twenty-eight now, crusty and impatient, a real hell-raiser whom most people found intimidating. Natalie had teased him and picked at him from her teens, and she still did. She adored him, despite his fiery temper and legendary impatience. A lot of that ill humor came from having one eye, and she knew it.

Soon after the accident that could as easily have killed him as blinded him, she told him that the rakish patch over his left eye made him look like a sexy pirate. He'd told her to go home and mind her own damned business. She ignored him and continued to help Vivian nurse him, even when he'd come home from the hospital. That hadn't been easy. Natalie was a senior in high school at the time. She'd just gone from the orphanage where she'd spent most of her life to her maiden aunt's house the year before the accident occurred. Her aunt, old Mrs. Barnes, didn't approve of Mack Killain, although she respected him. Natalie had had to beg to get her aunt to drive her first to the hospital and then to the Killain ranch every day to look after Mack. Her aunt had felt it was Vivian's job — not Natalie's — but Vivian couldn't do

9

a thing with her elder brother. Left alone, Mack would have been out on the northern border with his men helping to brand calves.

At first, the doctors feared that he'd lost the sight in both eyes. But later, it had become evident that the right one still functioned. During that time of uncertainty, Natalie had attached herself to him and refused to go away, teasing him when he became despondent, cheering him up when he wanted to quit. She wouldn't let him give up, and soon there had been visible progress in his recovery.

Of course, he'd tossed her out the minute he was back on his feet, and she hadn't protested. She knew him right down to his bones, and he realized it and resented it. He didn't want her for a friend and made it obvious. She didn't push. As an orphan, she was used to rejection. Her aunt hadn't taken her in until the dignified lady was diagnosed with heart failure and needed someone to take care of her. Natalie had gone willingly, not only because she was tired of the orphanage, but also because her aunt lived on Killain's southern border. Natalie visited her new friend Vivian most every day after that. It wasn't until her aunt had died unexpectedly and left her a sizeable nest egg that she'd been able to put herself through college and keep up the payments on the little house she and her aunt had occupied together.

She lived frugally, and she'd managed all by herself. The money was almost gone now, but she'd made good grades and she had the promise of a teaching position at the local elementary school when she graduated. Life at the age of twenty-two looked much better than life at age six, when a grieving child had been taken from her family home and placed in the orphanage after a fire had killed both her parents. Like Mack, she'd had her share of tragedy and grief.

But teaching was wonderful. She loved first graders, so open and loving and curious. That was going to be her future. She and Dave Markham, a sixth-grade teacher at the school, had been dating for several weeks. No one knew that they were more friends than a romantic couple. Dave was sweet on the clerk at the local insurance agency, who was mooning over one of the men she worked with. Natalie wasn't interested in marriage anytime soon. Her only taste of love had been a crush on an older teenager when she was in her senior year. He'd just started noticing her when he was killed in a wreck while driving home from an out-of-town weekend fishing trip with his cousin. Losing her parents, then the one love of her short life, had taught her the danger of loving. She wanted to be safe. She wanted to be alone.

Besides that, she was far too fastidious for the impulsive leap-into-bed relationships that seemed the goal of many modern young women. She had no interest in falling in love, or in a purely physical affair. So until Dave came along, she hadn't dated at all. Well, that wasn't quite true, she conceded.

There was the dance she'd coaxed Mack into taking her to, but he'd been far older than the boys at the local community college who had attended. Nevertheless, he'd made Natalie the belle of the ball just by escorting her. Mack was a dish, by anybody's standards, even if he did lack social graces. By the time they left, he'd put more backs up than a debating team. She hadn't asked him to take her anywhere else, though. He seemed to dislike everybody these days. Especially Natalie.

Natalie hadn't really minded his abrasive company. She admired his penchant for telling the truth even when it wasn't wel-

12

come, and for saying what he thought, not what was socially acceptable. She tended to speak her own mind, too. She'd learned that from Mack. He'd forced her to fight back soon after she became friends with his sister. He put her back up and kept it up, refusing to let her rush off and cry. He taught her to stand her ground, to have the courage of her convictions. He made her strong enough to bear up under almost anything.

She remembered that they had an argument the night she'd coaxed him to the dance. He'd left her at her front door with one poisonous remark too many, his black eye narrow and no smile to ease the hard, lean contours of his face. There was too much between them to let a disagreement keep them apart, though.

Mack looked much older than twenty-eight. He'd had so much responsibility on his broad shoulders that he'd been robbed of a real childhood. His mother had died young, and his father had succumbed to drink, and then became abusive to the kids. Mack had stood up to him, many times taking blows meant for the other three. In the end, their father had suffered a stroke and been placed in a nursing home while Mack kept the younger

13

Killains together and supported them by working as a mechanic in town. When Mack was twenty-one, his father had died, leaving Mack with three teenagers to raise.

Meanwhile, he'd invested carefully, bought good stock and started breeding his own strain of Red Angus. He was successful at everything he touched. His only run of real bad luck had been when he'd been thrown from his horse in the pasture with a big Angus bull. When the bull had charged him and he'd tried to catch it by the horns to save himself, he'd been gored in the face. He'd lost his sight, but fortunately only in one eye. The rest of him was still pure, splendid male, and women found him very appealing physically. He was every woman's secret desire, until he opened his mouth. His lack of diplomacy kept him single.

Natalie left Vivian crying in the living room and went to find Mack. He was on one knee in a stall on the cobblestones of the spacious, clean barn, ruffling the fur of one of his border collies. He was a kind man, for the most part, and he did love animals. Every stray in Baker County made a beeline for the Killain place, and there were always furry friends around to pet. The border collies were working dogs, of course, and used to help herd cattle on the vast plains. But Mack adored them, and it was mutual.

Natalie leaned against the doorway of the barn with her arms folded and smiled at the picture he made with the pup.

As if he sensed her presence, his head rose. She couldn't see his eyes under the shadow of his wide-brimmed hat, but she knew he was probably glaring at her. He didn't like letting people see how very human he was.

"Slumming, Miss Educator?" he drawled, rising gracefully to his feet.

She only smiled, used to his remarks. "Seeing how the other half lives, Mr. Cattle Rancher," she shot back. "Vivian says you won't let the love of her life through the front door."

"So what are you, a virgin sacrifice to appease me?" he asked, approaching her with that quick, menacing stride that made her heart jump.

"You aren't supposed to know that I'm a virgin," she pointed out when he stopped just an arm's length away.

He let out a nasty word and smiled mockingly, waiting to see what she'd say.

She ignored the bad language, refusing to rise to the bait. She grinned at him instead.

That disconcerted him, apparently. He pushed his hat over his jet black hair and stared at her. He had Lakota blood two generations back. He could speak that language as fluently as French and German. He took classes from far-flung colleges on the Internet. He was a great student; everything fascinated him.

His bold gaze roamed down her slender body in the neat, fairly loose jeans and soft yellow V-neck sweater she wore. She had short dark hair, very wavy, and emerald green eyes. She wasn't pretty, but her eyes and her soft bow mouth were. Her figure drew far more attention than she was comfortable with, especially from Mack.

"Viv's would-be boyfriend got the Henry girl pregnant last year," he said abruptly.

Her gasp made his eye narrow.

"You didn't have a clue, did you?" he mused. "You and Viv are just alike."

"I beg your pardon?"

"Pitiful taste in men," he added.

She gave him a look of mock indignation. "And I was just going to say how very sexy you were!"

"Pull the other one," he said with amazing coldness.

Her eyebrows arched. "My, we're touchy today!"

He glared at her. "What do you want? If it's an invitation to supper for Viv's heart-throb, he can't come unless you do."

That surprised her. He usually couldn't wait to shoo her off the place. "Three's a crowd?" she murmured dryly.

"Four. I live here," he pointed out. He frowned. "More than four," he continued. "Vivian, Bob and Charles and me. You and the would-be Romeo make six."

"That's splitting hairs," she pointed out. "You're suggesting that I come over to make the numbers even, of course," she chided.

His face didn't betray any emotion at all. "Wear a dress."

That really surprised her. "Listen, you aren't planning any pagan sacrificial rites at a volcano?" she asked, rubbing in the virgin sacrifice notion.

"Something low-cut," he persisted, his gaze narrow and faintly sensual on her pert breasts under the sweater.

"Stop staring at my breasts!" she burst out indignantly, crossing her arms over them.

"Wear a bra," he returned imperturbably.

Her face flamed. "I am wearing a bra!"

His black eye twinkled. "Wear a thicker bra."

She glared at him. "I don't know what's gotten into you!"

He lifted an eyebrow and his eye slid down her body appraisingly. "Lust," he said matter-of-factly. "I haven't had sex for so long, I'm not even sure I remember how."

She couldn't handle a remark like that. They shared such intimate memories for two old sparring partners. She couldn't fence with him verbally when he let his voice drop like that, an octave lower than normal. It was so sensuous that it made her knees weak. So was the memory of that one unforgettable night they'd shared. Warning signals shot to her brain.

He sighed theatrically when her cheeks turned pink. "So much for all that sophistication you pretend to have," he mused.

She cleared her throat. "I wish you wouldn't say things like that to me," she said worriedly.

"Maybe I shouldn't," he conceded. His hand went out and pushed a strand of hair behind her small ear. She jerked at his touch, and he moved a step closer. "I'd never hurt you, Natalie," he said quietly.

She managed a nervous smile. "I'd like that in writing," she said, trying to move away without making it look as if she was intimidated, even though she was.

The barn door was at her back, though, and there was no way to escape. He knew that. She could see it on his face as he slid one long arm beside her head and rested his hand by her ear.

Her heart jumped into her throat. She looked at him with all her darkest fears reflecting in her emerald eyes.

He searched them without speaking for a long moment. "Carl would never have made you happy," he said suddenly. "His people had money. They wouldn't have let him marry an orphan with no assets."

Her eyes darkened with pain. "You don't know that."

"I *do* know that," he returned sharply. "They said as much at the funeral, when someone mentioned how devastated you were. You couldn't even go to the funeral."

She remembered that. She remembered, too, that Mack had come looking for her in her aunt's home the night Carl had died. Her aunt was out of town shopping over the weekend, and she'd been all alone. Mack found her in a very sexy pink satin gown and robe, crying her eyes out. He'd picked her up, carried her to the old easy chair by the bed, and he'd held her in his lap until she couldn't cry anymore. After a close call that still made her knees weak, even in memory, he'd stayed with her that whole long, anguished night, sitting in the chair beside the bed, watching her sleep. It was a mark of the respect he commanded in the community that even Natalie's aunt hadn't said a word about his presence there when she found out about it on her return. Natalie inspired defense in the strangest quarters. Her tenderness made even the toughest people oddly vulnerable around her.

"You held me," she recalled softly.

"Yes." His face seemed to tauten as he looked at her. "I held you."

She felt him so close that it was like being lifted and carried away. Little twinges of pleasure shot through her when she met his searching gaze. The sensation was so intense as they looked at each other, she could almost feel his bare chest against hers. Five years had passed since that night, but it seemed like yesterday. It was like stepping into space.

"And when I lost my sight," he continued, "you held me."

She bit her lower lip hard to stop it from trembling. "I wasn't the only one who tried to nurse you," she recalled.

"Vivian cried when I snapped at her, and

the boys hid under their beds. You didn't. You snapped right back. You made me want to go on living."

She lowered her eyes to his chest. He had the build of a rodeo cowboy, broad-shouldered and lean-hipped. His checked shirt was open at the neck, and she saw the thick, curling hair that covered him from his chest to his belt. He wasn't a hairy man, but he was devastating without a shirt. She'd seen him like that more often than she was comfortable remembering. He was beautiful under his clothing, like a sculpture she'd seen in pictures of museum exhibits. She even knew how he felt, there where the hair was thick over his breast-bone. . . .

"You were kind to me when Carl died," she returned.

There was a new tension between them after she spoke. She sensed a steely anger in him.

"Since we're on the subject of your poor taste in men, what do you see in that Markham man?" he asked curtly. "He's as prissy as someone's maiden aunt, and in a stand-up fight, he'd go out in seconds."

She lifted her face. "Dave's my friend," she said shortly. "And certainly he's no worse than that refugee from the witch trials that you go around with!"

His firm lips pursed. "Glenna's not a witch."

"She's not a saint, either," she assured him. "And if you're going without sex, I can guarantee it's not *her* fault!" she added without thinking. But once the words left her stupid mouth, and she saw the unholy light in the eye that wasn't covered by the black eye patch, she could have bitten her tongue in two.

"Will you two keep your voices down?" young Bob Killain groaned, as he peered around the barn door to stare at them. "If Sadie Marshall hears you all the way in the kitchen, she'll tell everybody in her Sunday school class that you two are living in sin out here!" he exclaimed, naming the Killain housekeeper.

Natalie looked at him indignantly, both hands on her slender hips. "It's Glenna you'd better worry about, if he gets involved with her!" she assured Mack's youngest brother, a redhead. "Her name is written in so many phone booths, she could qualify as a tourist attraction!"

Mack tried not to laugh, but he couldn't help himself. He pulled his hat across his eyes at a slant and turned into the barn. "Oh, hell, I'm going to work. Haven't you got something to do?" he asked his brother.

Bob cleared his throat and tried desperately not to laugh, either. "I'm just going over to Mary Burns's house to help her with her trigonometry."

"Carry protection," Mack's droll voice came back to him.

Bob turned as red as his hair. "Well, we don't all stand around talking about sex all day!" he muttered.

"No," Natalie agreed facetiously. She looked at Mack deliberately. "Some of us go looking for names in phone booths and call them up for dates!"

"Can it, Nat," Mack said as he opened a stall and led a horse out. He proceeded to saddle it, ignoring Natalie and Bob.

"I'll be back by midnight!" Bob called, seeing an opportunity to escape.

"You heard what I said," Mack called after him.

Bob made an indignant sound and stomped out of the barn.

"He's just sixteen, Mack," she said, regaining her composure enough to join him as he fastened the cinch tight.

He glanced at her. "You were just seventeen when you were dating the football hero," he reminded her.

She stared at him curiously. "Yes, but except for a few very chaste kisses, there wasn't much going on."

He gave her an amused glance before he went back to his chore. He tested the cinch, found it properly tight and adjusted the stirrups.

"What does that look mean?" Natalie asked curiously.

"I had a long talk with him when I found out you'd accepted a date for the Christmas dance from him."

Her lips fell open. "You what?"

He slid a booted foot into the stirrup and vaulted into the saddle with easy grace. He leaned over the pommel and looked at Natalie. "I told him that if he seduced you, he'd have me to contend with. I told his parents the same thing."

She was horrified. She could hardly breathe. "Of all the interfering, presumptuous —"

"You were raised in an orphanage by spinster women, and then you lived with your aunt, who couldn't even talk about kissing without going into a swoon," he said, and he didn't smile. "You knew nothing about men or sex or hormones. Someone had to protect you, and there wasn't anybody else to do it."

"You had no right!"

His dark eye slid over her with something like possession. "I had more right than I'll ever tell you," he said quietly. "And that's all I'll say on the subject."

He turned the horse, deaf to her fury.

"Mack!" she raged.

He paused and looked at her. "Tell Viv she can have her friend over for supper Saturday night, on the condition that you come, too."

"I don't want to come!"

He hesitated for a minute, then turned the horse and came back to her. "You and I will always disagree on some things," he said. "But we're closer than you realize. I know you," he added in a tone that made her knees wobble. "And you know me."

She couldn't fight the emotions that made her more confused, more stirred, than she'd ever been before. She looked at him with eyes that betrayed her longing for him.

He drew in a long, slow breath, and his face seemed to lose its rigor. "I won't apologize for looking out for you."

"I'm not part of your family, Mack," she said huskily. "You can tell Viv and Bob and Charles what to do, but you can't tell me!"

He studied her angry face and smiled

gently, in a way that he rarely smiled at anyone. "Oh, I'm not telling, baby," he replied softly.

"And don't call me baby, either!"

"All that fire and fury," he mused, watching her. "What a waste."

She was so confused that she could hardly think. "I don't understand you at all today!"

"No," he agreed, the smile fading. He looked straight into her eyes, unblinking. "You work hard at it, too."

He turned the horse, and this time he kept riding.

She wanted to throw things. She couldn't believe that he'd said such things to her, that he'd come so close in the barn that for an instant she'd thought that he meant to kiss her. And not a chaste brush on the cheek, like at Christmas parties under the mistletoe, either. But a kiss like ones she'd seen in movies, where the hero crushed the heroine against the length of his body and put his mouth so hard against hers that she couldn't breathe at all.

She tried to picture Mack's hard, beautiful mouth on her lips, and she shivered. It was bad enough remembering how it had been that rainy night that Carl had died, when one thin strap on her nightgown had slid down her arm and . . .

26

Oh, no, she told herself firmly. Oh, no, none of that! She wasn't going to start daydreaming about Mack again. She'd gone down that road once already, and the consequences had been horrible.

She went back into the house to tell Viv the bad news.

"But that's wonderful!" her friend exclaimed, all smiles instead of tears. "You'll come, won't you?"

"He's trying to manipulate me," Natalie said irritably. "I won't let him do that!"

"But if you don't come, Whit can't come," came the miserable reply. "You just have to, Nat, if I'm your friend at all."

Natalie grumbled, but in the end, she gave in.

Vivian hugged her tight. "I knew you would," she said happily. "I can hardly wait until Saturday! You'll like him, and so will Mack. He's such a sweet guy."

Natalie hesitated, but if she didn't tell her friend, Mack certainly would, and less kindly. "Viv, did you know that he got a girl in trouble?"

"Well, yes," she said. "But it was her fault," she pointed out. "She chased him and then when they did it, she wouldn't let him use anything. He told me."

Natalie blushed for the second time that

day, terribly uncomfortable around people who seemed content to speak about the most embarrassing things openly.

"Sorry," Viv said with a kind smile. "You're very unworldly, you know."

"That's just what your brother said," Natalie muttered.

Vivian studied her curiously for a long time. "He may not like the idea of Whit, but he likes the idea of your friend Dave Markham even less," she confided.

"He's one to criticize *my* social life, while he runs around with the likes of Glenna the Bimbo. Stop laughing, it isn't funny!"

Vivian cleared her throat. "Sorry. But she's really very nice," she told her friend. "She just likes men."

"One after the other," Natalie agreed, "and even simultaneously, from what people say. Your brother is going to catch some god-awful disease and it will be his own fault. Why are you still laughing?"

"You're jealous," Vivian said.

"That'll be the day!" Natalie said harshly. "I'm going home."

"He's only gone out with her twice," her best friend continued, unabashed, "and he didn't even have lipstick on his shirt when he came home. They just went to a movie together."

28

"I'm sure your brother didn't get to his present age without learning how to get around lipstick stains," she said belligerently.

"The ladies seem to like him," Vivian said.

"Until he speaks and ruins his image," Natalie added. "His idea of diplomacy is a gun and a smile. If Glenna likes him, it's only because she's taped his mouth shut!"

Vivian laughed helplessly. "I guess that could be true," she confessed. "But he is a refreshing change from all the politically correct people who are afraid to open their mouths at all."

"I suppose so."

Vivian stood up. "Natalie?"

"What?"

She stared at her friend quietly. "You're still in love with him, aren't you?"

Natalie turned quickly toward the door. She wasn't going to answer. "I really have got to go. I have exams next week, and I'd better hit the books hard. It wouldn't do to flub my exams and not graduate," she added.

Vivian wanted to tell Natalie that she had a pretty good idea of what had happened between her and Mack so long ago, but it would embarrass Natalie if she came right out with it. Her friend was so repressed.

29

"I don't know what happened," she lied, "but you have to remember, you were just seventeen. He was twenty-three."

Natalie turned, her face pale and shocked. "He . . . told you?"

"He didn't tell me anything," Vivian said softly and honestly. She hadn't needed to be told. Her brother and her best friend had given it away themselves without a word. She smiled. "But you walked around in a constant state of misery and wouldn't come near the place when he was home. He wouldn't be at home if he knew you were coming over to see me. I figured he'd probably said something really harsh and you'd had a terrible fight."

Natalie's face closed up. "The past is best left buried," she said curtly.

"I'm not prying. I'm just making an observation."

"I'll come Saturday night, but only because he won't let Whit come if I don't," Natalie said a little stiffly.

"I'll never mention it again," Vivian said, and Natalie knew what she meant. "I'm sorry. I didn't mean to dredge up something painful."

"No harm done. I'd long since forgotten." The lie slid glibly from her tongue, and she smiled one last time at

Vivian before she went out the door. Pretending it didn't matter was the hardest thing she'd done in years.

Chapter 2

Natalie sat in the elementary school classroom the next morning, bleary-eyed from having been up so late the night before studying for her final exams. It was imperative that she read over her notes in all her classes every night so that when the exam schedule was posted, she'd be ready. She'd barely had time to think, and she didn't want to. She never wanted to remember again how it had been that night when she was seventeen and Mack had held her in the darkness.

Mrs. Ringgold's gentle voice, reminding her that it was time to start handwriting practice, brought her to the present. She apologized and organized the class into small groups around the two large class tables. Mrs. Ringgold took one and she the other as they guided the children through the cursive alphabet, taking time to study each effort and offer praise and corrections where they were necessary.

It was during lunch that she met Dave Markham in the line.

"You look smug today," he said with a smile. He was tall and slender, but not in the same way that Mack was. Dave was an intellectual who liked classical music and literature. He couldn't ride or rope and he knew next to nothing about agriculture. But he was sweet, and at least he was someone Natalie could date without having to worry about fighting him off after dessert on dates.

"Mrs. Ringgold says I'm doing great in the classroom," she advised. "Professor Bailey comes to observe me tomorrow. Then, next week, finals." She made a mock shiver.

"You'll pass," he said, smiling. "Everybody's terrified of exams, but if you read your notes once a day, you won't have any trouble with them."

"I wish I *could* read my notes," she confided in a low tone. "If Professor Bailey could flunk me on handwriting, I'd already be out on my ear."

"And you're teaching children how to write?" Dave asked in mock horror.

She glared at him. "Listen, I can tell people how to do things I can't do. It's all a matter of using authority in your voice."

"You do that pretty well," he had to admit. "I hear you had a good tutor."

"What?"

33

"McKinzey Killain," he offered.

"Mack," she corrected. "Nobody calls him McKinzey."

"Everybody calls him Mr. Killain, except you," he corrected. "And from what I hear, most people around here try not to call him at all."

"He's not so bad," she said. "He just has a little problem with diplomacy."

"Yes. He doesn't know what it is."

"In his tax bracket, you don't have to." She chuckled. "Are you really going to eat liver and onions?" she asked, glancing at his plate and making a face.

"Organ meats are healthy. Lots healthier than that," he returned, making a face at her taco. "Your stomach will dissolve from jalapeño peppers."

"My stomach is made of cast iron, thanks."

"How about a movie Saturday night?" he asked. "That new science fiction movie is on at the Grand."

"I'd love to . . . oh, I'm sorry, I can't," she corrected, grimacing. "I promised Vivian I'd come to supper that night."

"Is that a regular thing?" he wanted to know.

"Only when Vivian wants to bring a special man home," she said with a rueful smile. "Mack says if I don't come, her boy-friend can't come."

He gave her an odd look. "Why?"

She hesitated with her tray, looking for a place to sit. "Why? I don't know. He just made it a condition. Maybe he thought I wouldn't show up and he could put Viv off. He doesn't like the boy at all."

"Oh, I see."

"Where did all these people come from?" she asked, curious because there were hardly any seats vacant at the teachers' table.

"Visiting committee from the board of education. They're here to study the space problem," he added amusedly.

"They should be able to see that there isn't any space, especially now."

"We're hoping they may agree to budget an addition for us, so that we can get rid of the trailers we're presently using for class-rooms."

"I wonder if we'll get it."

He shrugged. "Anybody's guess. Every time they talk about adding to the millage rate, there's a groundswell of protest from property owners who don't have children."

"I remember."

He found them two seats at the very end of the teachers' table and they sat down to

35

the meal. She smiled at the visiting committee and spent the rest of her lunch hour discussing the new playground equipment the board of education had already promised them. She was grateful to have something to think about other than Mack Killain.

Natalie's little house was just on the outskirts of the Killain ranch, and she often complained that her yard was an afterthought. There was so little grass that she could use a Weed Eater for her yard work. One thing she did have was a fenced-in back yard with climbing roses everywhere. She loved to sit on the tiny patio and watch birds come and go at the small bird feeders hanging from every limb of her one tree — a tall cottonwood. Beyond her boundary, she could catch occasional glimpses of the red-coated Red Angus purebred cattle the Killains raised. The view outside was wonderful.

The view inside was another story. The kitchen had a stove and a refrigerator and a sink, not much else. The living-room-dining-room combination had a sofa and an easy chair — both second-hand — and a used Persian rug with holes. The bedroom had a single bed and a dresser, an old armchair and a straight chair. The porches were small and needed general repair. As homes went, it was hardly the American dream. But to Natalie, whose life had been spent in an orphanage, it was luxury to have her own space. Until her junior year, when she moved into her aunt's house to become a companion/nurse/housekeeper for the two years until her aunt died suddenly, she'd never been by herself much.

She had one framed portrait of her parents and another of Vivian and Mack and Bob and Charles — a group shot of the four Killains that she'd taken herself at a barbecue Vivian had invited her to on the ranch. She picked up the picture frame and stared hard at the tallest man in the group. He was glaring at the camera, and she recalled amusedly that he'd been so busy giving her instructions on how to take the picture that she'd caught him with his mouth open.

He was like that everywhere. He knew how to do a lot of things very well, and he wasn't shy with his advice. He'd walked right into the kitchen of a restaurant one memorable day and taught the haughty French chef how to make a proper barbecue sauce. Fortunately, the two of them had gone into the back alley before anything got broken.

She put the picture down and went to make herself a sandwich. Mack said she didn't eat right, and she had to agree. She could cook, but it seemed such a waste of time to go to all that trouble just for herself. Besides, she was usually so tired when she got home from her student teaching that she didn't have the energy to prepare a meal.

Ham, lettuce, cheese and mayonnaise on bread. All the essentials, she thought. She approved her latest effort before she ate it. Not bad for a single woman.

She turned on the small color television the Killains had given her last Christmas — a luxury she'd protested, for all the good it did her. The news was on, and as usual, it was all bad. She turned on an afternoon cartoon show instead. Marvin the Martian was much better company than anything going on in Washington, D.C.

When she finished her sandwich, she kicked off her shoes and curled up on the sofa with a cup of black coffee. There was nothing like having a real home, she thought, smiling as her eyes danced around the room. And today was Friday. She'd traded days with another checkout girl, so she had Friday and Saturday off from the grocery store she worked at part-time. The market was open on Sunday, but with a skeleton crew, and Natalie wasn't scheduled for that day, either. It would be a dream of a weekend if she didn't have to dress up and go over to the Killains' for supper the following night. She hoped Vivian wasn't serious about the young man she'd invited over. When Mack didn't approve of people, they didn't usually come back.

Natalie only had one good dress, a black crepe one with spaghetti straps, that fell in a straight line to her ankles. There was a lacy shawl she'd bought to go with it, and a plain little pair of sling-back pumps for her small feet. She used more makeup than usual and grimaced at her reflection. She still didn't look her age. She could have passed for eighteen.

She got into her small used car and drove to the Killain ranch, approving the new paint job Mack's men had given the fences around the sprawling Victorian home with its exquisite gingerbread wood-work and latticed porches. It could have slept ten visitors comfortably even before Mack added another wing to accommodate his young brothers' desire for privacy.

There was a matching garage out back where Mack kept his Lincoln and the big doublecabbed Dodge Ram truck he used on the ranch. There was a modern barn where the tractors and combine and other ranch equipment were kept, and an even bigger stable where Mack lodged his prize bulls. A separate stable housed the saddle horses. There was a tennis court, which was rarely used, and an Olympic-size indoor swimming pool and conservatory. The conservatory was Natalie's favorite place when she visited. Mack grew many species of orchids there, and Natalie loved them as much as he did.

She expected Vivian to meet her at the foot of the steps, but Mack came himself. He was wearing a dark suit and he looked elegant and perturbed with his hands deep in his pockets as he waited for her to mount the staircase.

"Don't you have another dress?" he asked irritably. "Every time you come over here, you wear that one."

She lifted her chin haughtily. "I work six days a week to put myself through college, pay for gas and utilities and groceries. What's left over wouldn't buy a new piece of material for a mouse suit."

"Excuses, excuses," he murmured. His

eyes narrowed on the low cleavage. "And I still don't like that neckline," he said shortly. "It shows too much of your breasts."

She threw up both hands, almost flinging her small evening bag against the ceiling. "Listen, what's this hang-up you have about my breasts lately?" she demanded.

He was frowning as he stared at her bodice. "You're flaunting them."

"I am *not!*"

"It's all right to do it around me," he continued flatly, "but I don't want Vivian's sex maniac boyfriend to start drooling over you at my supper table."

"I don't attract that sort of attention," she muttered.

"With a body like that, you'd attract attention from a dead man," he said shortly. "Just looking at you makes me ache."

She didn't have a comeback. He'd taken the sense right out of her head with that typically blunt remark.

"No sassy reply?" he taunted.

Her eyes ran over him in the becoming suit. "You don't look like a man with an ache."

"How would you know?" he asked. "You don't even understand what an ache is."

She frowned. "You're very difficult to understand."

"It wouldn't take an experienced woman five seconds to know what I meant," he told her. "You're not only repressed, you're blind."

Both eyebrows lifted. "I beg your pardon?"

He let out an angry breath. "Oh, hell, forget it." He turned on his heel. "Are you coming in or not?"

"You're testy as all get out tonight," she murmured dryly, following him. "What's wrong with you? Can't Glenna get rid of that . . . ache?"

He stopped and she cannoned into his back, almost tripping in the process. He spun around and caught her by the waist, jerking her right against him. He held her there, and one lean hand went to the small of her back and ground her hips deliberately into his.

He held her gaze while his body tautened and swelled blatantly against her stomach. "Glenna can't get rid of it because she doesn't cause it," he said with undeniable mockery.

"McKinzey Donald Killain!" she gasped, outraged.

"Are you shocked?" he asked quietly.

She tried to move back, but his hand contracted and he groaned sharply, so she stood very still in the sensual embrace.

"Does it hurt you?" she whispered huskily.

His breathing was ragged. "When you move," he agreed, a ripple running through his powerful frame.

She stared at him curiously, her body relaxing into the hard curve of him as both his hands went to her hips and held her there very gently.

He returned her quiet stare with his good eye narrowed, intent, searching her face. "I've never let you feel that before," he said huskily.

She was fascinated, not only with the intimacy of their position, but also with the strange sense of belonging it gave her to know that she could arouse him so easily. It didn't embarrass her, really. She felt possessive about him. She always had.

"Do you have this effect on Markham?" he asked, and he didn't smile.

"Dave is my friend," she replied. "It would never occur to him to hold me . . . like this."

"Would you let him, if he wanted to?"

She thought about that for a few seconds and she frowned again, worried. "Well, no," she confessed reluctantly.

"Why not?"

Her eyes searched his good one. "It would be . . . repulsive with him."

She felt his heartbeat skip. "Would it?" he asked. "Why?"

"It just would."

His lean hands spread blatantly over her hips and drew her completely against him. He shivered a little at the pleasure it sent careening through his body. His teeth ground together, and he closed his eyes as he bent to rest his forehead against hers.

Natalie felt her breasts go hard at the tips. Her arms were under his now, her hands flat against the rough fabric of his jacket. Her small evening bag lay somewhere on the wooden floor of the porch, completely forgotten. She felt, saw, heard nothing except Mack. Her whole body pulsated with delight at the feel of him so close to her. She could feel his minty breath on her lips while the sounds of the night dimmed to insignificance in her ears.

"Natalie," he whispered huskily, and his hands began to move her hips in a slow, sweet rotation against him. He groaned harshly.

She shivered with the pleasure. Her body rippled with delicious, dangerous sensations.

"Mack?" she whispered, lifting involuntarily toward him in a sensuous little rhythm.

His hands slid to her hips, her waist and blatantly over the thin fabric that covered her breasts in the lacy little long-line bra she wore under the dress. As she met his searching gaze, his hands went inside the deep V neckline and down over the silky skin of her breasts. She caught her breath at the bold caress.

"This," he said softly, "is a very bad idea."

"Of course it is," she agreed unsteadily. Her body was showing a will of its own, lifting and shifting to tease his lean hands closer to the hard tips that wanted so desperately to be caressed.

"Don't," he murmured quietly.

"Mack?"

His forehead moved softly against hers as he tried to catch his breath. "If I touch you the way you want me to, I won't be able to stop. There are four people right inside the house, and three of them would pass out if they saw us like this."

"Do you really think they would?" she asked in a breathless tone.

His thumbs edged down toward the tiny hardnesses inside the long-line and she whimpered.

45

"Do you want me to touch them?" he whispered at her lips.

"Yes!" she choked.

"It won't be enough," he murmured.

"It will. It will!"

"Not nearly enough," he continued. His mouth touched her eyelids and closed them while his thumbs worked their way lazily inside the lacy cups. "You have the prettiest little breasts, Natalie," he whispered as he traced the soft skin tenderly. "I'd give almost anything right now to put my mouth over them and suckle you."

She cried out, shocked at the delicious images the words produced in her mind.

"I ache," he breathed into her lips, even as his thumbs finally, *finally,* found her and pressed hard against the little peaks.

She sobbed, pushing her face against him as she shivered in the throes of unbelievable sensation.

He made a rough sound and maneuvered her closer to the dark end of the porch, away from the door and windows. His hands cupped her, caressed her insistently while his hot mouth pressed hungrily against her throat just where her pulse throbbed.

"Yes," she choked, lifting even closer into his hands. "Yes, Mack, yes, please, oh, please!"

"You crazy little fool!" he moaned.

Seconds later, he'd unzipped the dress and his mouth was where his hands had been, hot and feverish in its urgency as it sought the soft skin of her breast and finally forced its way into the lacy cup to fasten hungrily on the hard peak.

Her nails bit into the nape of his neck like tiny blades, pulling his mouth even closer as she fed on the exquisite demands it made on her innocence. She lifted against him rhythmically while he suckled her in the warm darkness, his arms contracted to bring her as close as he could get her.

The suddenness with which he pushed her away left her staggering, so weak that she could hardly stand. He'd moved away from her to lean against the wall, where one big hand pressed hard to support him. He was breathing as if he'd been running a race, and she could see the shudders that ran through his tall body. She didn't know what to say or what to do. She was overwhelmed. She couldn't even move to pull up her dress.

After a few seconds he took a harsh, deep breath and turned to look at her. She hadn't moved a step since he'd dragged himself away from her. He smiled ruefully.

She was, he thought, painfully innocent.

"Here," he said in a husky tone, moving to pull up her dress and fasten it. "You can't go inside like that."

She looked at him like a curious little cat while he dressed her, as if it was a matter of course to do it.

"Natalie," he laughed harshly, "you have to stop looking like an accident victim."

"Do you do that with her?" she asked, and her pale green eyes flashed.

He mumbled a curse as he fastened the hook at the top of the dress. "Glenna is none of your business."

"Oh, I see. You can ask me about my social life, and I can't ask you about yours, is that how it works?"

He frowned as he held her by both shoulders and looked at her. "Glenna isn't a fuzzy little peach ripening on a tree limb," he muttered. "She's a grown, sophisticated woman who doesn't equate a good time with a wedding ring."

"Mack!" Natalie exclaimed furiously.

"I don't even have to look at you to know you're blushing," he said heavily. "Twenty-two, and you haven't really aged a day since I held you in your bedroom the night of Carl's wreck."

"You looked at me," she whispered.

His hands tightened. "Lucky you, that looking was all I did."

Her eyes searched his face in the dim light. "You wanted me," she said with sudden realization.

"Yes, I did," he confessed. "But you were seventeen."

"And now I'm twenty-two."

He sighed and smiled. "There isn't much difference," he murmured. "And there still isn't any future in it."

"Not for a man who just wants to have a little fun occasionally," she said sarcastically.

"You certainly don't fall into that category," he agreed. "I've got two brothers and a sister to take care of here. There isn't room for a wife."

"Okay. Just forget that I proposed."

His fingers trailed gently across her soft, swollen mouth. "Besides the responsibilities, I'm not ready to settle down. Not for years yet."

"I'm sure they'll take back the engagement ring if I ask them nicely."

He blinked. "Are we having the same conversation?"

"I only bought you a cheap engagement ring, anyway," she continued outrageously.

49

"It probably wouldn't have fit, so don't worry about it."

He started laughing. He couldn't help it. She really was a pain in the neck. "Damn it, Natalie!" He hugged her close and hard, an affectionate hug with bare overtones of unsatisfied lust.

She hugged him back with a long sigh, and her eyes closed. "I think it's like baby ducks," she murmured absently.

"What is?"

"Imprinting. They follow the first moving thing they see when they hatch, assuming it's their mother. Maybe it's like that with men and women. You were the first man I was ever barely intimate with, so I've imprinted on you."

His heart jumped wildly and his arms tightened around her. "The world is full of men who want to get married and have kids."

"And I'll find one some day," she finished for him. "Have it your own way. But if you really want me to find someone else to fixate on, I have to tell you that dragging me into dark corners and pulling my dress half off isn't the way to go about it."

He was really laughing now, so hard that he had to let her go. "I give up," he said helplessly.

"It's too late now," she returned, going to fetch her purse from the floor. "You've said you don't want the ring."

"Let's go inside while there's still time," he replied as he moved toward the door.

"Not yet," she said quickly. She moved into a patch of light and looked into her compact mirror, taking time to replace her lipstick and fix her hair.

He watched her calmly, his gaze narrow and intense.

She put the compact in her evening bag and moved toward him. "You'd better do some quick repairs of your own," she murmured after she examined his face. "That shade of lipstick definitely doesn't suit you."

He gave her a glare, but he pulled out his handkerchief and let her remove the stains from his cheek and neck.

Fortunately, the lipstick had missed his white collar or there wouldn't be any disguising it.

"Next time, don't put on six layers of it before you come over here," he advised coolly.

"Next time, keep your hands in your pockets."

He chuckled dryly. "Fat chance, with your dress showing off your breasts like that."

She unfastened her lacy shawl and draped it across her bodice and over her shoulder. She gave him a haughty glance and waited for him to open the front door.

"The next dress I buy will have a mandarin neckline, you can bet on that," she told him under her breath.

"Make sure it doesn't have buttons, then," he whispered outrageously as he stood aside to let her pass.

"Lecher," she whispered.

"Temptress," he whispered back.

She walked past him and into the living room before he could think up any more smart remarks to throw at her. She looked calm, but inside, she was rippling with tiny fears and remnants of pleasure from his touch. It occurred to her that, over the years, she'd been more intimate with him than any other man she'd ever known, but he'd never kissed her.

Thinking about that didn't help her situation, so she smiled warmly at Bob and Charles as they rose to their feet, and then at Vivian and the tall, blond man who stood up from his seat on the sofa beside her.

"Natalie, this is Whit," Vivian introduced them. Her blue eyes looked at the blond man with total possession. Whit, in

52

turn, looked at Natalie as if he'd just discovered oil.

Oh, boy, Natalie thought miserably as she registered the gleam in Whit's blue eyes when they shook hands. He held hers for just a few seconds too long, and she grimaced. Here was a complication she hadn't counted on.

Chapter 3

It didn't help matters that Whit was a graduate of the same community college Natalie attended and had taken classes with some of the professors who taught her. Vivian had never wanted to go to college, and was unsure what she wanted to do with her life. Just recently, Mack had put his foot down and insisted that she get either a job or a degree. Vivian had been horrified, but she'd finally agreed to try a course in computer programming at the local vocational school. That was where she'd met Whit, who taught English there.

As they ate dinner, Natalie carefully maneuvered the conversation toward the vocational school, so that Vivian could join in. Vivian was livid and getting more upset by the minute. Natalie could have kicked Mack for putting her in this position. If only he'd let Vivian invite Whit over unconditionally!

"Why didn't you go to college to study computer programming?" Whit asked

Vivian, and managed to make it sound condescending.

"The classes were already full when I decided to go," Vivian said with a forced smile. "Besides, I'd never have met you if I'd gone to college instead of the vocational school."

"I suppose not." He smiled at her, but his attention went immediately back to Natalie. "What grade do you plan to teach?"

"First or second," Natalie said. "And I have to leave very soon, I'm afraid. I have exams next week, so I expect to be up very late tonight studying."

"You can't even stay for dessert?" Whit asked.

"Nope . . . sorry."

"What a shame," Whit said.

"Yes, what a shame." Vivian echoed the words, but the tone was totally different.

"I'll walk you out to your car," Mack said before Whit could volunteer.

Whit knew when he was beaten. He smiled sheepishly and asked Vivian if she'd pour him a second cup of coffee.

It was pitch black outside. Mack held Natalie's arm on the way down the steps, but not in any affectionate way. He was all but cutting off the circulation.

55

"Well, that was a disaster," he said through his teeth.

"It was your disaster," she pointed out irritably. "If you hadn't insisted that I come over, too —"

"Disaster is my middle name lately," he replied with halfhearted amusement.

"He isn't a bad man," she told him. "He's just normal. He likes anything with a passable figure. Sooner or later, Viv is going to realize that he has a wandering eye, and she'll drop him. *If*," she added forcibly, "you don't put her back up by disapproving of him. In that case, she'll probably marry him out of spite!"

He stopped at the driver's side of her car and let her arm fall. "Not if you're around, she won't."

"I won't be around. He gives me the willies," she said flatly. "If I hadn't had this shawl on, I'd have pulled the tablecloth over my head!"

"I told you not to wear anything low-cut."

"I only did that to spite you," she admitted. "Next time, I'll wear an overcoat." She dug in her evening bag for her car keys. "And I thought you said he was a boy. He isn't. He's a teacher."

"He's a boy compared to me."

"Most men are boys compared to you," she said impatiently. "If Viv used you as a yardstick, she'd never date anybody at all!"

He glared at her. "That doesn't sound very much like a compliment."

"It isn't. You expect anything male to be just like you."

"I'm successful."

"Yes, you're successful," she conceded. "But you're a social disaster! You open your mouth, and people run for the exits!"

"Is it my fault if people can't do their jobs properly?" he shot back. "I try not to interfere unless I see people making really big mistakes," he began.

"Waitresses who can't get the coffee strong enough," she interrupted, counting on her fingers. "Bandleaders who don't conduct with enough spirit, firemen who don't hold the hoses right, police officers who forget to give turn signals when you're following them, little children whose shoelaces aren't tied properly —"

"Maybe I interfere a little," he defended himself.

"You're a walking consumer advocate group," she countered, exasperated. "If you ever get captured by an enemy force, they'll shoot themselves!"

He started to smile. "Think so?"

She threw up her hands. "I'm going home."

"Good idea. Maybe the English expert will follow suit."

"If he doesn't, you could always correct his grammar," she suggested.

"That's the spirit."

She opened the door and got into the car.

"Don't speed," he said, leaning to the open window, and he wasn't smiling. "There's more than a little fog out here. Take your time getting home, and keep your doors locked."

"Stop nursemaiding me," she muttered.

"You do it to me all the time," he pointed out.

"You don't take care of yourself," she replied quietly.

"Why should I bother, when you're so good at doing it for me?" he queried.

She was losing the battle. It did serve to keep her mind off the way he'd held her earlier, the touch of those strong hands on her bare flesh. She had to stop thinking about it.

"Keep next Friday night open," he said unexpectedly.

She frowned. "Why?"

"I thought we might take Vivian and the

professor over to Billings to have dinner and see a play."

She hesitated. "I don't know . . ."

"What's your exam schedule?"

"One on Monday, one on Tuesday, one on Thursday and one on Friday."

"You'll be ready to cut loose by then," he said confidently. "You can afford one new dress, surely?"

"I'll buy myself some chain mail," she promised.

He grinned. It changed him, made him look younger, more approachable. It made her tingle when he looked like that.

"We'll pick you up about five."

She smiled at him. "Okay."

He moved away from the car, waiting until she started it and put it in gear before he waved and walked toward the porch. She watched him helplessly for several seconds. There had been a shift in their relationship. Part of her was terrified of it. Another part was excited.

She drove home, forcing herself not to think about it.

That night, Natalie had passionate, hot dreams of herself and Mack in a big double bed somewhere. She woke sweating and couldn't go back to sleep. She felt guilty enough to go to church. But when she got home and fixed herself a bowl of soup for lunch, she started thinking about Mack again and couldn't quit.

The rain was coming down steadily. If the temperature had been just a little lower, it might have turned to snow, even this late in the spring. Montana weather was unpredictable at best.

She got out her biology textbook and grimaced as she tried to read her notes. This was her second course on the subject, and she was uncomfortable about the up-coming exam. No matter how hard she studied, science just went right through her head. Genetics was a nightmare, and animal anatomy was a disaster. Her pro-fessor warned them that they'd better spend a lot of time in the lab, because they were going to be expected to trace blood flow through the various arteries and veins and the lymphatic system. Despite the extra hours she'd put in with her small lab study group, she was tearing her hair out trying to remember everything she'd learned over the course of the semester.

She'd been hard at it all afternoon when there was a knock at the front door. It was almost dark, and she was hungry. She'd have to find something to eat, she supposed. Halfway expecting Vivian, she went to the door barefooted, in jeans and a loose button-up green shirt with no makeup on and her hair uncombed. She opened the door and found Mack there, dressed in jeans and a yellow knit shirt, carrying a bag of food.

"Fish and chips," he announced.

"For me?" she asked, surprised.

"For us," he countered, elbowing his way in. "I came to coach you."

"You did?" She was beginning to feel like a parrot.

"For the biology exam," he continued. "Or don't you need help?"

"I'm considering around-the-clock prayer and going to class on crutches for a sympathy concession from my professor."

"I know your professor, and he wouldn't feel sorry for a dismembered kitten if it was trying to get out of his exam," he returned. "Do I get to stay?"

She laughed softly. "Sure."

He went into the kitchen and started getting down plates.

"I'll make another pot of coffee," she volunteered. She felt a little shy of him after the night before. They had such intimate memories for two old sparring partners. She glanced at him a little nervously as she went about the ritual of making coffee. "Wasn't your science fiction show on tonight?" she asked, because she knew he only watched one, and this was the night it ran.

"It's a rerun," he said smoothly. "Have you got any ketchup?"

"You're going to put ketchup on fish?" she asked in mock surprise.

"I don't eat things I can't put ketchup on," he replied.

"That lets out ice cream."

He tossed her a grin. "It's good on vanilla."

"Yuck!"

"Where's your sense of adventure?" he taunted. "You have to experience new things to become well rounded."

"I'm not eating ketchup on ice cream, whether it rounds people out or not."

"Suit yourself." He put fish and chips onto the plates, fished out two napkins and put silverware at two places on the small kitchen table.

"I gather we're eating in here," she murmured dryly.

"If we eat in the living room, you'll want to watch television," he pointed out. "And if you can find a movie you like, the studying will be over."

"Spoilsport."

"I want you to graduate. You've worked too hard, too long to slack off at the eleventh hour."

"I guess you know all about genetics?" she sighed, seating herself while the coffee finished dripping.

"I breed cattle," he reminded her. "Of course I do."

She grimaced. "I love biology. You'd think I'd be good at it."

"You're good with children," he said, smiling gently at her. "That's what matters the most."

She shrugged. "I suppose you're right." She studied his lean, dark face with its striking black eye patch. "Are you still half buried in Internet college courses?"

"Yes. It's forensic archaeology this semester. Bones," he clarified. His eye twinkled. "Want to hear all about it?"

"Not over fish and chips," she said distastefully.

"Squeamish, are you?"

"Only when I'm eating," she replied. She glanced at the coffeemaker, noted that the brewing cycle was over and got up to fill two thick white mugs with black coffee. She put his in front of him and seated herself. Neither of them took cream or sugar, so there was no sense in putting them on the table.

"How's Viv?" she asked as they started on the fish.

"Fuming. Lover boy went home without asking her for another date." He gave her a curious look. "She thought he might have phoned you."

"Not a chance," she said easily. "Besides, he's not my type."

"What is? The Markham man?" That was pure venom in his deep voice.

"Dave is nice."

"Nice." He finished a bite of fish and washed it down with coffee. "Am I nice?" he persisted.

She met his teasing glance and made a face at him. "You and a den of rattle-snakes."

"That's what I thought." He munched on a chip, leaning back in his chair to give her a long, steady scrutiny. "You're the only woman I know who improves without makeup."

"It's too much work when I'm home alone. I wasn't expecting company," she added.

He smiled. "I noticed. How old is that blouse?"

"Three years," she said with a sigh, noting the faded pattern. "But it's com-fortable."

His gaze lingered on it just a little too long, narrow and vaguely disturbing.

"I am wearing a bra!" she blurted.

His eyebrows lifted. "Are you really?" he asked in mock surprise.

"Don't stare."

He only smiled and finished his fish, oblivious to her glare.

"Tell me about blood groups," he said when they were on their second cup of coffee.

She did, naming them and describing which groups were compatible and which weren't.

"Not bad," he said when she was through. "Now, let's discuss recessive genes."

She hadn't realized just how much material she'd already absorbed until she started answering questions on those topics. It was only when they came to the formulae for the various combinations and the descriptions of genetic populations and gene pools that she foundered.

They went into the living room. She handed him the book. He stretched out on the sofa, slipping off his boots so that he could sprawl while she curled up in the big armchair across from him.

He read the descriptions to her, made

her recite them, then formulated questions to prompt the right answers. She couldn't remember being drilled so competently on a subject before.

Then he took her lab report and had her point out the various circulation patterns of blood through the body of a lab rat the class had dissected. He drew her onto the floor with him and put the book in front of them, so that she could see the diagram and label the various organs as well as the major arteries and veins.

"How does he do this on the exams?" he asked. "Does he lay out a diagram and have you fill in the spaces?"

"No. He usually just sticks a pin in the organ or vein or artery he wants us to identify."

"Barbarian," he muttered.

She grinned. "That's what we call him when he isn't listening," she admitted. "Actually, we have a much more thorough course of study in biology than most of the surrounding colleges, because most of our students go on to medical school or into nursing. Biology is a real headache here, but none of our students ever have to take remedial courses later on."

"That says a lot for the quality of teaching."

She smiled. "So it does."

He went over the anatomy schematic with her until she knew the answers without prompting. But it was ten o'clock when she started to yawn.

"You're tired," he said. "You need a good night's sleep, so you can feel up to the exam in the morning."

"Thanks for helping me."

He shrugged. "What are neighbors for?" he asked with a chuckle. "How about a cup of hot chocolate before I go home?"

"I'll make it."

He stretched lazily on the carpet. "I was hoping you'd offer. I can't make it unless I have something you just stir into hot milk. As I recall, you can do it from scratch."

"I can," she said smugly. "Won't take a jiffy."

She got down the ingredients, mixed them, heated the milk in her used microwave oven and took two steaming mugs into the living room. He was still sprawled on the carpet, so she sprawled with him, both of them using the sofa for a backrest while they drained the warm liquid.

"Just the thing to make me sleep," she murmured drowsily. "As if I needed help!"

"Do you think you know the material now?" he asked.

"Inside out," she agreed. "Thanks."

"You'd do the same for me."

"Yes, I would."

He finished his drink and put the mug on the side table, taking hers when she emptied it and placing it beside his.

"How do you feel about the other exams?" he asked.

"That material, I do know," she told him. "It was just a question of reviewing my notes every day. But this biology was a nightmare. I never thought I'd grasp it. You have a knack for making it sound simple. It isn't."

"I use a lot of it in my breeding program," he said on a lazy stretch. He flexed his shoulders. "You can't get good beef cattle unless you breed for specific qualities."

"I guess not." Her eyes went involuntarily to his high cheekbones, his straight nose, and then down to that disciplined, very sensuous mouth. It made her tingle to look at it.

"You're staring," he murmured.

"I was just thinking," she replied absently.

"Thinking what?"

She shifted a little and lowered her eyes, smiling shyly. "I was thinking that you've never kissed me."

"That's a lie," he returned amusedly. "I kissed you last Christmas under the mistletoe."

"That was a kiss?" she drawled.

"It was the only sort of kiss I felt comfortable with, considering that my brothers and my sister were staring at us the whole time," he said with a twinkle in his dark eye.

"I guess they'd run you ragged if you made a serious pass at someone."

"I've made several serious passes at you," he replied, and he didn't smile. "You don't seem to notice them."

She colored, and her voice felt choked. "I notice them, all right."

"You run," he corrected. His gaze fell to her soft mouth and lingered there. "I'd enjoy kissing you, Nat," he added quietly. "But a kiss is a stepping-stone. It leads down a road you may not want to walk right away."

She frowned, puzzled. "What sort of road?"

"I don't want to get married," he said simply. "And you don't want to have intercourse."

"McKinzey Killain!" she exclaimed, outraged, sitting straight up.

"There's another word for it." He

grinned wickedly. "Want to hear it?"

"You say it, and I'll brain you with your own boot!" she threatened, making a grab for one of the highly polished pair lying just past his hip.

He was too quick for her. He caught her arm as it reached his abdomen and jerked her down on the other side of him, turning her under a long, powerful leg and arm with speed and grace.

She found herself flat on her back looking into his taut, somber face. She'd expected laughter, amusement, even mocking good humor. None of those emotions was evident. He was very still, and his good eye held an intimidating expression.

She could feel the powerful muscle of his thigh across hers, the pressure vaguely arousing. She could feel the hard, heavy beat of his heart against her breasts in their light covering. She could taste his breath on her mouth as he stared at her from point-blank range. She began to feel hot and swollen all over from the unfamiliar proximity. She didn't know whether to try to laugh it off or fight her way off the carpet.

He seemed to sense her internal struggle, because that long leg moved enough to pin her in a position that was just shy of intimate.

She jerked and moved her hips. He caught them with one big, lean hand and held her down hard.

"Don't do that," he said huskily, "unless you're in a reckless mood."

She stilled, curious.

He let go of her hip and slid his hand into her hair, tugging off the band that held it in place behind her ears. He smoothed her hair over the carpet and looked into her face with an expression that bordered on possession.

His fingers trailed down the side of her neck to the opening of her blouse and lingered there, tracing a deliberate pattern on the soft skin that provoked a shiver from her responsive body.

His long leg moved, just barely, and her lips parted on an audible sound as her body arched involuntarily.

His hips shifted, pinning her, and his face hardened. "Do you know what that does to me? Or are you experimenting?"

She swallowed, and her eyes searched his. "I don't know what it does," she confessed huskily. "I feel very odd."

"Odd how?"

His intent gaze made her heartbeat

quicken. "I feel swollen," she whispered, as if she were telling him a secret.

His gaze dropped to her parted mouth. "Where?" he breathed. "Here?" And his hand slid under her hips and lifted her right into the blatant contours of his aroused body.

She did gasp then, but she didn't try to get away. She looked straight at him, enthralled.

"I want you," he said in a rough whisper. "And now you know what happens when I want you." His hand contracted, grinding her against him. "You'd better be sure what *you* want, before I go over the edge."

Her body seemed to dissolve under him. She made a husky little sound deep in her throat and shivered as delicious sensations rippled through her body.

He groaned. His hand moved into the thick fall of her hair and pinned her head as he bent down. "I should be shot," he ground out against her parted lips.

"Why?" she moaned, lifting her arms around his neck.

"Nat . . ."

The sound went into her mouth. He kissed her with a barely leashed hunger that made every secret dream of her life come true. She relaxed under him, reached up to hold him tight, moved her legs to admit the harsh downward thrust of his hips. She moaned again, a sound almost of anguish, as the kiss grew harder and slower and more insistent. He tasted of hot chocolate and pure man as he explored her soft, willing mouth. She'd been kissed, but never like this. He knew more about women than she ever expected to learn about men. She matched his hunger with enthusiasm rather than experience, and he knew immediately that she was in over her head.

He lifted his mouth, noticing with reluctant pleasure that she followed its ascent, trying to coax it back over her lips.

"No," he whispered tenderly, holding her down with a gentle arm right across her hard-tipped breasts.

"Why not?" she asked miserably. "Don't you like kissing me?"

He drew in an unsteady breath and ground his hips against hers. "Does that feel as if I like it?" he asked with black humor.

She just looked at him, a little shy but totally without understanding.

He shifted so that he was beside her on the carpet, arched across her yielding, taut body. "I don't keep anything in my wallet to use," he said bluntly. "If you want to make love, I have to go to town and buy something to keep you from getting pregnant. Does that make it any clearer?"

Her eyes seemed to widen impossibly for a few seconds. "You mean . . . have sex?"

"A man has sex with a one-night stand. You're not one."

She studied him quietly, with open curiosity. "I'm not?"

He traced her mouth with a lean forefinger, watching it open hungrily. "I want you very badly," he whispered. "But your conscience would beat you to death, with or without precautions."

She still hesitated. "Maybe . . ."

He put his finger across her lips. "Maybe not," he said with returning good humor. "I came over to teach you biology, not reproduction."

"You don't want babies," she said, and she sounded sad.

He grimaced. "I don't want them right now," he corrected. "One day, I'd like several." He traced her thin eyebrows lazily. "You haven't had much experience with men."

"I'm doing my best to learn," she murmured dryly.

His fingers trailed into her hair and

speared into its softness. "I'll tell you what to do, when the time comes. This isn't it," he added only half humorously.

She eyed him mischievously. "Are you sure?" She moved deliberately and smiled as he shuddered.

He caught her hip and held her down. "I'm sure," he resigned.

"Okay." She sighed and relaxed into the carpet. "I guess I can live on dreams if I have to."

He pursed his lips. "Do you dream about me?"

"Emphatically," she confessed.

"Should I ask how you dream about me?"

"I'll spare you the blushes," she told him, and moved away so that she could sit up. She pushed back her disheveled hair.

"So they're that sort of dreams, are they?" he asked, chuckling.

"I don't suppose you dream about me," she fished.

He didn't say anything for a long moment. Finally, he sat up and got to his feet gracefully. "I'm leaving while there's still time," he said, and he grinned at her.

"Craven coward," she muttered. "You'd never make a teacher. You have no patience with curious students."

75

"You've got enough curiosity for both of us," he told her. "Walk me to the door."

"If I must."

He paused with the door open and looked down at her with open possession. "One step at a time, Nat," he said softly. "Slow and easy."

She blushed at the tone and the soft insinuation.

He bent and brushed his mouth briefly against hers. "Get some sleep. I'll see you Friday."

"We're still going to Billings?"

"I wouldn't miss it for the world," he said gently. "Good night."

Frustrated and weak in her knees, she watched him stride to his car. She didn't know how it was going to work out, but she knew that there was no going back to the old easy friendship they'd once enjoyed. She wasn't sure if she was glad or not.

Chapter 4

There were plenty of nervous faces and anxious conversations when Natalie sat in the biology classroom to wait for the professor to hand out the written test questions. She'd assumed that the lab questions would require everyone to file into the lab with another sheet of paper and identify the labeled exhibits there. But the professor announced that the dissection questions were on a separate sheet included with the exam. Everybody was on edge. It was common knowledge that many people failed the finals in this subject and had to retake the course. Natalie prayed that she wouldn't. She couldn't graduate with her class if she flubbed it.

When the papers were handed out, the professor gave the go-ahead. Natalie read each question carefully before she began to fill in the tiny circles of the multiple choice questions. As she studied the drawing of the dissected rat and noted the placement of the various marks, she found that she remembered almost every single one. She was certain that she was going to pass the course. Mack had made sure of it. She almost whooped for joy when she turned in her paper and pencil. There was one more thing required — she had to fill out a rating sheet for the professor and the course, a routine part of finals. She loved the class and respected the professor, so her answers were positive. She turned in that sheet, too, and left the room. There were still fifteen people huddled over their papers when she went out the door, with only five minutes left for completion.

She almost danced to her car. One down, she thought delightedly. Three to go. And then, graduation! She could hardly wait to share her good news with Mack.

The week went by very quickly. Natalie was almost certain to graduate, because she knew she did well on her finals. The only real surprise would be her final grade, and it would include the marks she received for her practice teaching. She hoped her scores would be good enough to satisfy the school where she would begin her career next term.

When Friday rolled around, she breathed a sigh of relief as she left the English classroom where she'd finished her final round of questions. It was like being freed from jail, she reflected. Although she would miss her classmates and her professors, it had been a long four years. She was ready to go out into the world.

She hadn't heard from Mack all week. Vivian called her Thursday night to ask if she was still planning to go out with them. She didn't sound very enthusiastic about the double date. Natalie tried to smooth it over, but she knew that her friend was jealous, and she didn't know what to do about it. She must discuss it with Mack, she decided.

She tried his cell phone, and he answered with a voice that held both terse authority and irritation.

"Mack?" she asked, surprised by the tone, which he never used with her.

"Nat?" The impatience was gone immediately. "I thought you'd have forgotten this number by now," he added in a slow, smooth tone that sounded amused. "What do you want?"

"I need to talk to you."

There was a pause. She heard him cover the mouthpiece and talk to someone in the tone she'd heard when he first answered the phone. Then his voice came back to her. "Okay. Go ahead."

"Not over the phone," she said uncomfortably.

"All right. I'll come over."

"But I'm ready to leave," she protested. "I have to drive to town to buy a dress for tonight."

There was a pause. "Good for you."

"It's your fault. You keep making fun of the only dress I've got."

"I'll pick you up in ten minutes," he said.

"I told you, I'm going —"

"I'm going with you," he said. "Ten minutes."

The line went dead. Oh, no, she thought, foreseeing disaster. He'd have the women in the clothing store standing on their heads, and before he was through, the security guards would probably carry him out in a net.

But she realized it wasn't going to be easy to thwart him. Even if she jumped in her car and left, he knew where she was going. He'd simply follow her. It might be better to humor him. After all, she didn't have to buy a dress today. She could wear the one he didn't like.

He drew up in front of the door exactly ten minutes later, pushing the passenger door open when she came out of the house and locked it.

His dark gaze traveled over her neat figure in gray slacks and a gray and white patterned knit top. He wasn't wearing chaps or work boots. She assumed he'd been instructing his men on how to work cattle instead of helping with roundup. He looked clean and unruffled. She was willing to bet his men didn't.

"How many of your men have quit since this morning?" she asked amusedly after she'd fastened her seat belt.

He gave her a quick glare before he pulled the big, double-cabbed truck out of her driveway and into the ranch road that led to the highway. "Why do you think anyone quit?"

"It's roundup," she pointed out. She leaned against the door and studied him with a wicked grin. "Somebody always quits. Usually," she added, "it's the man who thinks he knows more than you do about vaccinations and computer-chip ear tags."

He made an uncomfortable movement and gave her a piercing glance before his foot went down harder on the accelerator. She noticed his boots. Clean and nicely polished.

"Jones quit," he confessed after a minute. "But he was going to quit anyway," he added immediately. "He thinks he knows too much about computer technology to waste it on a cattle ranch."

"You corrected him about the way he programmed your computer," she guessed.

He glared at her. "He did it wrong," he burst out. "What the hell was I supposed to do, let him tangle my herd records so that I couldn't track weight-gain ratios at all?"

She chuckled softly. "I get the picture."

He took off his gray Stetson and stuck it into the hat carrier above the visor. Impatient fingers raked his thick, straight black hair. "He was lumping the calves with the other cattle," he muttered. "They have to be done separately, or the data's no use to me."

"Had he ever worked on a ranch?"

"He worked on a pig farm," he said, and looked absolutely disgusted.

She hid a smile. "I see."

"He said the sort of operation didn't matter, that he knew enough about spreadsheet programs that it wouldn't matter." He glanced at her. "He didn't know anything."

"Ah, now I remember," she teased. "You took the computer programming courses *last* semester."

"I passed with honors," he related.

82

"Something *he* sure as hell didn't do!"

"I hope you never take a course in teaching," she said to herself.

"I heard that," he shot at her.

"Sorry."

He paused at the highway to make sure it was clear before he turned onto it. "How did exams go?"

"Much better than I expected," she said with a smile. "Thanks for helping me with the biology test."

He smiled. "I enjoyed it."

She wasn't sure how to take that, and when he glanced at her with a sensuous smile, she flushed.

"What sort of dress are you going to buy?" he asked.

She gave him a wary look. "I want a simple black one."

"Velvet's in this season," he said carelessly. "You'd look good in green velvet. Emerald green."

"I don't know . . ."

"I like the feel of it in my hands."

Her eyes narrowed and she glared at him. "Oh, does Glenna wear it?" she asked before she thought.

"No." He studied her for as long as he dared take his gaze off the highway. He smiled. "I like that."

"You like what?" she asked irritably.

"You're jealous."

Her heart skipped a beat. She stared out the window, searching for a defense.

"It wasn't a complaint," he said after a minute.

"I still don't want to be anyone's mistress, in case you were wondering," she said blatantly, hoping to distract him. She was jealous — she just didn't want to admit it.

He chuckled. "I'll keep that in mind."

It was a short drive. She told him where she wanted to go, and he pulled the truck into a parking space near the door of the small boutique.

"You don't have to come in, too," she protested when he joined her on the sidewalk.

"Left to your own devices, you'll come out carrying a black sack with shoulder straps. Where you go, I go," he said imperturbably. "Think of me as a fashion consultant."

She glared at him, but he didn't budge. "All right," she gave in. "But don't you start handing out advice to the saleslady! If you do, I'm leaving."

"Fair enough."

He followed her into the shop, where a

young woman and an older one were browsing through dresses on a sale rack.

As Natalie headed in that direction, he caught her hand gently in his and maneuvered her to the designer dresses.

"But I can't . . ." she began.

He put his forefinger across her soft mouth. "Come on."

He gave her a considering look and moved hangers until he found a mid-calf-length velvet dress with cape sleeves and a discreet V neckline. He pulled it out, holding it up to Natalie's still body. "Yes," he said quietly. "The color does something for your eyes. It makes them change color."

"Why, yes, it does," an elderly saleslady said from behind him. "And that particular model is on sale, too," she added with a smile. "We ordered it for a young bride who became unexpectedly pregnant and had to bring it back."

Natalie looked at the dress and then at Mack with uncertainty in her face.

"It's okay," he murmured drolly. "Pregnancy isn't contagious."

The saleslady had to turn away quickly. The younger woman across the shop couldn't help herself and burst out laughing.

"Try it on," he coaxed. "Just for fun."

She clasped it to her chest, turned and followed the saleslady to the back of the store where the fitting rooms were located.

How Mack had judged the size so correctly, she didn't want to guess. But it was a perfect fit, and he was absolutely right about the way it changed her eyes. It made her look mysterious, seductive, even sexy. Despite her lack of conventional beauty, it gave her an air of sophistication. She looked pretty, she thought, surprised.

"Well?" he asked from outside the fitting room.

She hesitated. Oh, why not, she asked herself. She opened the stall door and walked into the shop.

Mack didn't say anything. He didn't have to. His whole face seemed to clench as he studied her seductive young body in the exquisite garment that fit her like a custom-made glove.

"Well?" she asked, echoing his former query.

His gaze went up to collide with hers. He didn't say a word. His hands were in his pockets, and he didn't remove them. He couldn't seem to stop looking at her.

"It was made for you, my dear," the saleslady said with a sigh.

"We'll take it," Mack said quietly.

"But, Mack, I'm not sure . . ." she began. There hadn't been a price tag on the garment, and even on sale, it might be more than her budget could stand.

"I am." He turned on his heel and followed the sales-lady out of the fitting room.

Natalie looked after them wistfully. She could protest, but Mack and the saleslady had just formed a team that the Dallas Cowboys couldn't defeat. She gave in.

By the time Natalie changed into her slacks and shirt and tidied her hair with a small brush from her purse, Mack was signing a sales slip. He handed it to the sales-lady along with the pen, and turned as Natalie emerged with the dress over her arm.

"Let me have it, dear, and I'll hang it for you."

Natalie gave it up, watching blankly as the saleslady put it on a hanger, draped a bag over it and tied the bag at the bottom.

"I hope you enjoy it," the saleslady said with a smile as she handed the hanger to Mack.

"Thank you," Natalie said, uncertain if she was thanking the saleslady or her determined escort.

Mack led her out of the store and put

her in the truck after he'd hung her new dress on the hook in the back seat.

"Do you need shoes to go with it?" he asked.

"I have some nice black patent leather ones, and a purse to match," she said. "Mack, how could you pay for it? Everyone will think —"

His hand caught hers and curled into it hungrily. "Nobody will know you didn't buy it yourself unless you tell them," he said curtly. His head turned and he looked at her intently. "It really was made for you."

"Well . . ."

His fingers curled intimately into hers. "You can wear it to Billings," he said. "And when we go nightclubbing."

Her heart raced madly, as much from the caressing touch of his strong fingers as from what he said. "Are we going nightclubbing?"

"We're going lots of places," he said casually. "You don't start teaching until fall. That means, you'll have plenty of spare time. We can go on day trips and picnics, too."

Her body tingled from head to toe. She looked at the big, beautiful hand holding hers. "All four of us?" she asked, wondering if he wasn't taking this chaperon thing a little too seriously.

"You and me, Nat."

"Oh."

He turned off the highway onto a dirt track that led under an enormous pecan tree. He stopped and cut off the engine. The dark eye that met hers was somber and intent on her face.

"Are you serious about Markham?" he asked at once.

"I told you before, he's my friend."

"What sort of friend?" he persisted. "Do you kiss him?"

She frowned worriedly. "Well, no . . ."

"Why not?"

She sighed angrily. "Because I don't like kissing him. Mack . . ."

"You like kissing me," he continued quietly.

"You're making me nervous," she blurted. "I don't understand why you're asking so many questions all of a sudden."

He unfastened his seat belt and then hers before he pulled her across his body, her back to the steering wheel and her head resting on his left shoulder. He looked at her for a long moment before he spoke.

"I want to know if you have any long-

range plans that involve your teaching col-
league," he said finally.

"Not the sort you mean," she confessed.

His lean hand traced her shoulder and
then slid down sensuously right onto her
soft, firm breast. She gasped and caught
his wrist, but he wouldn't budge.

"You don't have to pretend to be outraged," he said gently. "I've touched you
like this before."

"You shouldn't," she whispered, flustered.

"Why not?" His hand spread in a slow,
sensuous caress that made her nipples go
immediately hard. "Your body likes it, even
if your mind doesn't."

"My body is stupid," she muttered.

"No, it isn't. It has excellent taste in
men," he mused, tongue in cheek.

"Will you be reasonable? It's broad daylight. What if someone drives down this
way?" she asked, exasperated.

"We'll tell them a bee got in your blouse
and I stopped to take it out," he murmured
as his head lowered. "Now stop worrying
about slim possibilities and kiss me."

She tried to tell him that it wasn't a good
idea, but his mouth was already firmly on
her soft lips before she could get a word
out. He nibbled at her upper lip in a lazy,

sensual rhythm that made it difficult for her to think. When his hand slid inside the blouse and under the strap of the flimsy lace bra, she stopped thinking altogether.

She heard the soft moan of the wind outside and the closer sound of her heartbeat in her ears. She curled a hand into Mack's cotton shirt and lifted herself closer to him.

He bit her lower lip gently while his fingers felt for buttons and moved them out of buttonholes before he coaxed her soft hand inside his shirt and against warm, hard muscle and thick black hair.

It brought back memories of the rainy night he'd come to sit with her after Carl was killed. He'd held her close in his arms that night, too, and he'd pulled her hands inside his shirt, against his bare chest. She remembered his sudden, frightening loss of control. . . .

Her hand stilled against him as she drew her mouth from under his and looked at him with traces of apprehension in her drowsy eyes.

"What's wrong?" he asked.

She swallowed. "I don't want to . . . to make things difficult for you," she said finally.

"They're already difficult." He shifted

her in his arms so that her head lay in the crook of his arm, and his hand went under her blouse and around her to unfasten the hooks on her bra.

"We shouldn't," she tried to protest.

He lifted his head and looked around for a few seconds before his gaze came back to her. "There isn't a car in sight," he said. "And I'm not planning to ravish you within sight of a major highway."

"I knew that."

"Tell me you don't want this and I'll let you go," he said bluntly, hesitating.

She wanted to. She really did. He looked impossibly arrogant with his shirt half un-buttoned and his mouth swollen from the long, hard contact with her lips. His hair was mussed by her fingers, and he looked somber and dangerous. She should tell him to let her go. But his fingers were tracing under her arm, and her traitorous body was writhing in an attempt to get his hand where she really wanted it. She could barely breathe as she twisted helplessly against him.

"That's what I thought," he said quietly, and he shifted her again, just enough to give him room to pull the blouse and bra up, baring her breasts to his intent scru-tiny.

Natalie couldn't get enough breath to make a token protest. She loved letting him look at her. She loved the slow, gentle tracing of his fingertips on her delicate skin. She loved the way he looked at her, as if she were a work of art. It wasn't possible to be ashamed.

"Nothing to say?" he teased softly.

"Nothing at all," she whispered, her breath jerking with the little bites of pleasure he gave her with his tender exploration of her breasts.

His thumb moved roughly over her nipple, and she bit her lower lip as pure delight arched her against him.

"I've never felt with anyone the things I feel with you," he breathed as his head lowered. "Some nights, I think I'll go stark raving mad from just the dreams."

She barely heard him. His mouth suddenly covered her breast, and he suckled her, hard.

The cry she made was audible. She trembled as he fed on her soft, smooth skin. It was cool in the cab of the truck, but she was burning all over. Her arms looped around his neck, and she hid her hot face in his neck as the pressure of his mouth increased until it almost made her weep with pleasure.

She pulled at his head, trying to get his mouth even closer, but he pulled back, his eye stormy as it met hers.

"Don't," he said gently. "You'll make me hurt you."

"It won't hurt me." She shivered. Her eyes were as turbulent as the emotions that were overwhelming her. "Don't stop," she whispered unsteadily.

His fingers traced the curve of her breast, and he looked down to watch her body lift up against them.

"Your skin is like silk," he said huskily. "I can't get enough of it." He bent again, his hard mouth smoothing over her in a caress that made her moan.

She arched up, totally without inhibitions, loving his warm lips on her body.

The sound of a car in the distance brought his head up reluctantly. He glanced at the highway, grimaced and helped her sit. "I thought we were alone on the planet," he murmured with a forced laugh. "I suppose it was wishful thinking. Need any help?" he asked as she fumbled behind her for catches.

"I can do it." She glanced at the car as it whizzed past. So much for isolation, she thought, and flushed when she realized how embarrassed she would have been if the car had pulled in behind them and stopped instead of going on its way.

He watched her loop her seat belt across her chest and fasten it. He did the same with his before he cranked the truck.

"A woman like you could make a man conceited," he said with a tender smile.

"It isn't my fault that I can't resist you," she pointed out. "And if you'd stop undressing me —"

"I can't do that," he interrupted. "I'd have nothing left to live for." He backed up until he could pull onto the highway. "Besides," he added with a grin, "how would you ever get any practical experience?"

"I think I may be getting too much," she replied. Her eyes slipped over him possessively, but she looked away before he noticed.

"Don't worry," he said. "I won't push you into doing something you don't really want."

"Do you think you could?"

"I know I could," he replied quietly. "But you'd hate me for it. Maybe I'd hate myself. Whatever happens, it has to be honest and aboveboard. No sneak attacks or seduction."

"I won't sleep with you," she said defensively.

"You would, but I'm not going to let it go that far between us. I've got as much responsibility as I can handle already." His face seemed to harden before her eyes. "The boys can take care of themselves, but Viv can't. She seems to get less mature by the day." He glanced at her. "And she's poisonously angry at you right now."

"Because Whit paid me too much attention, I gather," she said miserably.

"Exactly."

"But that wasn't my fault," she muttered.

"I know that. Vivian won't believe it. Have you forgotten how she was just after Carl was killed?" he added. "She never considered you his girlfriend. She swore he only dated you to get near her. I love my sister, but she has enough conceit for two women."

"Vivian is really beautiful," she pointed out. "I'm not."

He looked at her and smiled slowly. "You're worth any ten beauty queens, Nat," he said in a tone that was like being stroked with a velvet glove. "You have a big heart and you're kind. Too kind, sometimes. You can't refuse people, and they take advantage of you."

"Yes, I noticed," she said pointedly. "Just because I let you kiss me —"

"Stop while you're ahead," he cautioned with a bland look. "That was as mutual a passion as any two people ever shared. You love having my mouth on your body. You can't even hide it."

She crossed her legs and glared out the window with her arms folded. "I don't know beans about men, so I'm a pushover."

"Really? Then why won't you let the fellow teacher touch you?"

She gave him a hard glare, which he ignored. "You came along when I was at an impressionable age," she reminded him. "Remember what I said about baby ducks and imprinting?"

"You're no baby duck."

"I'm imprinted, just the same," she said angrily. "Seventeen years old, and spoiled for other men in the course of a night. You should never have come near me while I was in such a vulnerable state!"

"I couldn't leave you by yourself to grieve," he pointed out. "And you may have been vulnerable, but you didn't protest very much."

"You didn't leave me enough breath to protest with," she reminded him. "I may have been stupid about men, but you were no novice! I was outflanked and out-gunned!"

"I'm sorry about Carl, but you were no match for him. He liked a more flighty sort of girl altogether, and he had no plans to marry until he finished college. You'd have broken your heart over him."

"It was my heart to break."

He stopped at a traffic light and turned to meet her angry eyes. "For an intelligent woman, you are unbelievably naïve. Did you really think he took you out because he was in love with you?"

"He was," she said. "He told me he was!"

"He told his friends that he dated you because his brother bet him he couldn't get you to go out with him. There was more to it than that," he added somberly, "but I'll spare you the rest."

"How do you know what he was planning?" she demanded, outraged.

"His younger brother and Bob were good friends," he reminded her. "When Bob got wind of it, he came to me. That's why I had words with Carl and his parents before he tried anything with you."

She was devastated. She'd mourned Carl for months when she was seventeen, and now it turned out that he'd only dated her on a dare. He hadn't loved her. He'd been playing a game. She leaned her head against her window and bit back tears. She was a bigger fool than she'd realized. Why hadn't she guessed? And why hadn't Mack told her years ago?

Chapter 5

Mack saw the glitter of tears in her eyes and he grimaced. "I'm sorry," he said tersely. "I should never have told you."

She pushed back a wisp of hair and dug in her purse for a tissue so she could wipe her eyes. "You should have told me years ago," she corrected. "What an idiot I was!"

"You were naïve," he said gently. "You saw what you wanted to see."

His face was grim, and she realized belatedly that he was angry. She wondered what else Carl had said to his brother, but she was leery of asking.

He glanced at her and tapped his fingers on the steering wheel. "You were seventeen and bent on putting him on a pedestal for life. It would have been a waste."

That note in his voice was almost defensive. She turned in the seat and looked at him openly. She was seeing things she didn't want to see. "What you did . . . that night," she faltered. "It was deliberate."

"It was," he confessed quietly. "I wanted

to give you something to think about, at least something to compare with what you'd already experienced." His jaw tensed. "I didn't realize how innocent you were until it was too late."

"Too late?"

He slowed for a turn and he looked so formidable that she didn't say another word. A tense silence lay between them for several long seconds.

"Maybe it really was like imprinting," he said heavily. "I should never have touched you. You were far too young for what happened."

She felt her face coloring. The hungry passion they'd shared today and the night at his house was almost as explosive as what they'd shared all those years ago. Even in memory, her body burned as she relived her first experience of Mack.

"Do you think I blame you?" she asked finally, but she didn't look at him.

"I blame myself. You've lived like a recluse ever since."

She leaned her face against the glass of the window and smiled. "You were a pretty hard act to follow," she said huskily.

His hands tightened on the steering wheel. "So were you." He sounded as if the words were dragged out of him, and she turned her head to encounter a stare that stopped her heart.

It was as if she could see right into his mind, and she ached at the images that flashed at her, memories they shared.

"I didn't really expect that you'd be inexperienced just because I warned your boyfriend off," he added after a minute. "I got the shock of my life when I realized that you'd never experienced even the mildest form of intimacy."

"Men always say they know, but how do they?" she asked irritably.

He forced his gaze to the road. "Because of the way you reacted," he said tersely. "A sophisticated woman gives as much as she gets, Nat," he told her bluntly. "You were wide-eyed and fascinated by everything I did, and I got in over my head long before I expected to. I dreamed about that night for years."

"If we're making confessions, so did I," she admitted without looking at him.

He grimaced. "I should have gone home before I gave in to temptation."

Her pale eyes touched his face like loving hands. She'd never known anyone like him. She didn't think there was anyone else like him. He'd colored her dreams, become her world, in the years since that one incredible night.

She didn't answer him. He glanced at her and laughed hollowly. "Which doesn't change the past or bring us any closer to a solution," he mused. "You're not liberated, and I'm a confirmed bachelor."

She toyed with her seat belt. "Are you really? I used to think that your father made you wary of marriage. He and your mother were totally unsuited, from what everybody says."

"Everybody being my sister, Vivian," he guessed. "She doesn't remember our mother."

"Neither do you, really, do you?" she wondered aloud.

"She died and left him with four kids," he told her. "He wasn't up to raising even one. I've always thought that the pressure of it started him drinking, and then he couldn't stop."

His face hardened with the words, and she knew he was remembering the bad times he'd had with his father.

"Mack, do you really think you're like him?" she asked softly.

"They say abused kids become abusive parents," he replied without thinking, and then could have bitten his tongue right through for the slip.

She only nodded, as if she'd expected that answer. "So they say. But there are exceptions to every rule. If you were going to be abusive, Vivian and Bob and Charles would have been sitting in the school counselor's office years ago. They could have asked to go into foster care any time they wanted to."

"Vivian would never have given up shopping sprees," he pointed out.

She swiped gently at his sleeve. "Stop that. You know she loves you. So do the boys. You're the kindest human being I've ever known."

A ruddy color ran up his high cheekbones. He didn't look at her. "Flattery?"

"Fact," she countered. Her fingers smoothed over his sleeve lazily. "You're one of a kind."

He moved his shoulder abruptly. "Don't do that."

She pulled her fingers back. "Okay. Sorry." She laughed it off, but her face flushed.

"Don't get your feelings hurt," he said irritably, glancing at her. "I want you. Don't push your luck."

Her eyes widened.

"You still haven't got the least damned notion of what it does to me when you touch me, do you?" he asked impatiently. "This stoic exterior is a pose. Every time I look at you, I see you in that velvet dress, and I want to stop the truck and . . ." He ground his teeth together. "It's been a long dry spell. Don't make it worse."

"What about Glenna?" she chided.

He hesitated for a minute and then glanced at her with a what-the-hell sort of smile and said, "She can't fix what she didn't break."

Her eyebrows reached for the ceiling. "You don't look broken to me."

"You know what I mean. She's pretty and responsive, but she isn't you."

Her face brightened. "Poor Glenna."

"Poor Dave What's-his-name," he countered with a mocking smile. "Apparently he doesn't get any further with you than she does with me."

"Everyone says he's very handsome."

"Everyone says she's very pretty."

She shook her head and stared out the window, folding her arms. "Vivian is barely speaking to me," she said, desperate to change the subject. "I know she's jealous of the way Whit flirts with me. I just don't know how to stop him. It almost seems as if he's doing it deliberately."

"He is," he said, his expression changing.

"It's an old ploy, but it's pretty effective."

"I don't understand."

He pulled up at a stop sign a few miles outside Medicine Ridge and looked at her. "He makes her think he isn't interested so that she'll work harder to attract his attention. By that time, she's so desperate that she'll do anything he wants her to do." His eye narrowed angrily. "She's rich, Nat. He isn't. He makes a good salary, for a teacher, but I had him investigated. He spends heavily at the gambling parlors."

She bit her lower lip. "Poor Viv."

"She'd be poor if she married him," he agreed. "That's why I object to him. He did get a girl in trouble, but that's not why I don't want him hanging around Viv. He's a compulsive gambler and he doesn't think he has a problem." He looked genuinely worried. "I haven't told her."

She whistled softly. "And if you do tell her . . ."

"She won't believe me. She'll think I'm being contrary and dig in her heels. She might marry him out of spite." He shrugged. "I'm between a rock and a hard place."

"Maybe I should encourage him," she began.

"No."

"But I could —"

"I said no," he repeated, his tone full of authority. "Let me handle it my way."

"All right," she said, giving in.

"I know what I'm doing," he told her as he pulled the truck onto the highway. "You just be ready at five."

"Okay, boss," she drawled, and grinned at his quick glare.

Natalie was on pins and needles waiting for five o'clock. She was dressed by four. She'd topped her short hair with a glittery green rhinestone hair clip that brought out the emerald of her eyes and made the green velvet dress look even more elegant. When the Lincoln pulled up in her front yard and Mack got out to meet her on the porch, she fumbled trying to lock her door.

He took her hand in his and held it tight. "Don't start getting flustered," he chided gently, looking elegant in his dinner jacket and matching slacks. The white shirt had only the hint of ruffles down the front, with its black vest and tie. He was devastating dressed up. Apparently he found her equally devastating, because his glance swept over her from the high heels to the crown of her head. He smiled.

"You look nice, too," she said shyly.

His fingers locked into hers. "I'm rather glad we aren't going to be alone tonight," he murmured dryly as they walked toward the car. "In that dress, you'd tempt a carved statue."

"I'm not taking it off for you," she told him. "You're a confirmed bachelor."

"Change my mind," he challenged.

Her heart jumped and she laughed. "That's a first."

"Tonight is a first," he pointed out as they paused beside the passenger door. He looked at her with slow, sensuous appraisal. "Our first date, Natalie."

She colored. "So it is."

He opened the door. In the back seat, Vivian and Whit broke apart quickly, and Vivian laughed in a high-pitched tone, pushing back her short blond hair.

"Hi, Nat!" Vivian said cheerfully, sounding totally unlike the very stressed woman who'd phoned her the day before. "You look terrific."

"So do you," Natalie said, and her friend really was a knockout in pale blue silk. Whit was wearing evening clothes, like Mack, but he managed to look slouchy just the same. Vivian didn't notice. She was clinging to Whit's arm as if he was a treasure she was fearful of losing.

"I have a black velvet dress, but I wanted something easier to move around in," Vivian said.

"Velvet's very nice," Natalie agreed.

"Very expensive, too," Vivian added, as if she knew that Natalie hadn't paid for the dress.

"They do have charge accounts, even for penniless college students," Natalie pointed out in a tone she rarely used.

Vivian flushed. "Oh. Of course."

"We aren't all wealthy, Vivian," Whit added in a cooler tone. "It's nice for you, if you can pay cash for things, but we lesser mortals have to make do with time payments."

"I said I'm sorry," Vivian said tightly.

"Did you? It didn't sound very much like it," Whit said and moved away from her.

Vivian's teeth clamped shut almost audibly, and she grasped her evening bag as if she'd like to rip it apart.

"Which play are we going to see?" Natalie asked quickly, trying to recover what was left of the evening.

"*Arsenic and Old Lace*," Mack said.

"The Billings community college drama classes are presenting it. I've heard that they are pretty good."

"Medicine Ridge College has a strong drama department of its own, doesn't it, Natalie?" Whit asked conversationally. "I took a class in dramatic arts, but I was always nervous in front of an audience."

"So was I," Natalie agreed. "It takes someone with less inhibitions than I have."

"I had the lead in my senior play," Vivian said coldly.

"And you were wonderful," Natalie said with a smile. "Even old Professor Blake raved about your portrayal of Stella."

"Stella?" Whit asked.

"In Williams's play *A Streetcar Named Desire*," Natalie offered.

"One of my favorites," Whit said, turning to Vivian. "And you played the lead. You never told me that!"

Vivian's face lit up magically, and for the next few minutes, she regaled Whit with memories of her one stellar performance. In the front seat, Natalie and Mack exchanged sly smiles. With any luck, Natalie's inspiration could have saved the evening.

The play was hilarious, even if Natalie did find herself involuntarily comparing the performances with those of Cary Grant and Raymond Massey in the old motion picture. She chided herself for that. The actors in the play might be amateurs, but they were very good and the audience reacted to them with hysterical laughter.

Afterward, they went to a nightclub for a late supper. Natalie and Mack ordered steak and a salad, while Whit and Vivian managed to pick the most expensive dishes on the menu.

There was dancing on the small floor with a live band, a Friday night special performance, and Natalie found herself in Mack's arms as soon as she finished the last spoonful of her dessert.

"This is worth waiting all day for," he murmured in her ear as he held her close on the dance floor. "I knew this dress would feel wonderful under my hands."

She snuggled closer. "I thought Viv was going to ask how I could afford it," she said with a sigh. She closed her eyes and smiled. "You really shouldn't have paid for it, you know."

"Yes, I should have." He made a turn, and her body was pushed even closer to his. She felt his body react with stunning urgency to the brush of hers. She faltered and almost fell.

"Sorry," she said shakily.

He only laughed, the sound rueful and faintly amused as they continued across the floor. "It's an unavoidable consequence lately with you," he murmured. "Don't worry. No one will notice. We're alone here."

She glanced past his chest at the dozen or so other couples moving lazily to the music and she laughed, too. "So I see."

"Just don't do anything reckless," he said softly.

"With very little effort, we could become the scandal of the county."

She felt his lips at her forehead and smiled. "Think so?"

One lean hand was at the back of her head, teasing around her nape and her ears in a sensual exploration that made her tingle all over. "Do you remember what I told you the night of the wreck?" he asked huskily.

"You told me a lot of things," she hedged.

"I told you that, when you were old enough, I'd teach you everything you need to know about men." His hand slid to her waist and pulled her gently closer. "You're old enough, Nat."

She stiffened. "You stop that," she whispered urgently, embarrassed by his blatant capability.

"Sorry. It doesn't work that way. I'd need a cold shower, and that isn't going to happen here." His cheek brushed against hers and his lips touched just the corner of her mouth. "We could drop Vivian and the professor off at my house first," he said under his breath.

Her heart ran wild. "And then what?"

His lips traced her earlobe. "We could do what we did that night. I've spent years dreaming about how it felt."

Her knees threatened to collapse. "Mack Killain," she groaned. "Will you please stop?"

"You can't stop an avalanche with words," he whispered roughly. "You burn in me like a fever. I can't eat, sleep, think, work, because you're between me and every single thing I do."

She swallowed. "It's just an ache," she said firmly. "Once you satisfied it, where would we be?"

He drew back a little and looked into her eyes evenly. "I don't think it can be satisfied," he said through his teeth.

She stood very still, like a doe in the glare of bright headlights, looking at him.

"And you still don't know what it feels

113

like," he said gruffly, in a tone that was just short of accusation. "You like being kissed and touched, but you don't know what desire is."

She averted her eyes. "You're the one who always pulls back," she said huskily.

His arm contracted roughly, pinning her to him. "I have to," he said impatiently. "You have no idea what it would be like if I didn't."

"I'm twenty-two," she reminded him. "Almost twenty-three. No woman reaches that age today, even in a small town, without knowing something about relationships."

"I'm talking about physical relationships. They aren't something you have and walk away from. They're addictive." He drew in a harsh breath as the music began to wind down. "They're dangerous. A little light lovemaking is one thing. What I'd do to you in a bed is something else entirely."

The tone, as much as the content, made her uneasy. She stared at him, frowning. "I don't understand."

He groaned. "I know. That's what's killing me!"

"You're not being rational," she murmured.

The hand at her waist contracted and

moved her in a rough, quick motion against the rock-solid thrust of his body. He watched her blush with malicious pleasure. "How rational does that feel to you?" he asked outrageously.

She forced her eyes to his drawn face. "It isn't rational at all. But you keep trying to save me from anything deep and intimate. It has to happen someday," she said.

His jaw tautened even more. "Maybe it does. But I told you, I'm not a marrying man. That being the case, I'd have to be out of my mind before I'd take you to bed, Natalie."

"Dave wouldn't," she taunted. "In fact, Whit wouldn't," she added, glancing at Vivian's partner, who was watching her as much as he was watching his partner.

His hand tightened on her waist until it hurt. "Don't start anything with him," he said coldly. "Vivian would never forgive you. Neither would I."

"I was just kidding."

"I'm not laughing," he told her, and his face was solemn.

"You treat me like a child half the time," she accused, on fire with new needs. She felt reckless, out of control. His body, pressed so close to hers, was making her ache. "And then you accuse me of tempting you, when you're the one with the experience."

He let her go abruptly and moved back. "You aren't old enough for me," he said flatly.

"I'm six years younger than you are, not twenty," she pointed out.

His eye narrowed, glittering at her. "What do you want from me?"

In his customary blunt way, he'd thrown the ball into her court and stood there arrogantly waiting for an answer she couldn't give.

"I want you to be my friend," she said finally, compromising with her secret desires.

"I am."

"Then where's the problem?"

"You just felt it."

"Mack!"

He caught her hand and tugged her toward their table.

"What's that song — one step forward and two steps back? That's how I feel lately."

She felt churned up, frustrated, hot with desire and furious that he was playing some sort of game with her hormones. She knew she was flushed and she couldn't quite meet Vivian's eyes when they went to the table.

"Don't sit down," Whit drawled, catching Natalie by the wrist before she could be seated. "This one's mine."

He drew her on the dance floor to the chagrin of brother and sister and wrapped her tight as the slow dance began.

"If you want to keep that arm, loosen it," Natalie told Whit with barely contained rage.

He did, at once, and grinned at her. "Sorry. That's the way big brother was holding you, though. But, then, he's almost family, isn't he? Vivian says the two of you went through high school together."

"Yes, we did. We've been friends for a long time."

"She's jealous of you," he said.

"That's a hoot," she replied, laughing. "She's a beauty queen and I'm plain."

"That isn't what I mean," he corrected. "She envies you your kind heart and intelligence. She has neither."

"That's a strange way to talk about a girl you care for," she chided.

"I like Vivian a lot," he said. "But she's like so many others, self-centered and spoiled, waiting for life to serve up whatever she wants. I'll bet there hasn't been a man in years who's said no to her."

"I don't think anyone's ever said no to

her," she replied with a smile. "She's pretty and sweet, whatever else she is."

He shrugged. "Pretty and rich. I guess that's enough for most men. When do you start teaching?"

"In the fall, if I passed my exams. If I don't graduate, it will be another year before I can get a teaching job around here."

"You could go farther afield," he told her. "I was surfing the Internet the other night, browsing for teachers' jobs. There are lots of openings in north Texas, especially in Dallas. I always thought I'd like to live in Texas."

"I don't really want to live that far from home," she said.

"But you don't have a home, really, do you?" he asked. "Vivian said you were orphaned when you were very young."

"My mother was born here," she said. "So was her mother, and her mother's mother. I have roots."

"They can be a trap as much as a safety cushion," he cautioned. "Do you really want to spend the rest of your life out here in the middle of nowhere?"

"That's an odd question for someone who came here from Los Angeles," she pointed out.

He averted his gaze. "Nevada, actually,"

he said. "I got tired of the rat race. I wanted someplace quiet. But it's just a little too quiet here. A year of it is more than I expected to do."

"Do you like teaching?"

He made a face. "Not really. I wanted to do great things. I had all these dreams about building exotic houses and making barrels of money, but I couldn't get into architecture. They said I had no talent for it."

"That's a shame."

"So I teach," he added with a cold smile. "English, of all things."

"Viv says you're very good at it."

"It doesn't pay enough to keep me in decent suits," he said in a vicious tone. "When I think of how I used to live, how much I had, it makes me sick."

"What did you do before you were a teacher?" she asked, fishing delicately.

"I was in real estate," he said, but he didn't meet her eyes. "It was a very lucrative business."

"Couldn't you get a license here in Montana and go back into it?"

"Nobody wants to buy land in Montana these days," he muttered. "It's not exactly hot real estate."

"I suppose not."

The music ended and he escorted her to

the table, where Mack and Vivian sat fuming.

Vivian got to her feet at once. "And now it's my turn," she said pertly and with a smile that didn't quite reach her eyes.

"Sure," Whit said easily, and smiled as he led her onto the dance floor.

"What was all the conversation about?" Mack wanted to know.

"I was trying to draw him out about his former profession. He said he was in real estate in Nevada," she said, with a wary glance toward Viv and Whit, who were totally involved with each other for the moment.

"And I'm the tooth fairy," Mack said absently.

Natalie laughed helplessly.

"What?" he demanded.

"I was picturing you in a pink tutu."

That eye narrowed. "You'll pay for that one."

"Okay. A white tutu."

He shook his head. "Finish your drink. We have to leave pretty soon. I have an early appointment in town tomorrow."

"Okay, boss," she drawled, and ignored his stormy expression.

As it turned out, Mack took Natalie home first and walked her to her front door. "Try to stay out of trouble," he cautioned. "I may see you at the grocery store tomorrow."

"Sadie shops. You don't."

"I can shop if I want to," he said. He searched her bright face. "Just for the record, I wanted to take them home first."

She smiled. "Thanks."

One shoulder lifted and fell. "It isn't the right time. Not yet." He bent and brushed a soft kiss against her forehead. "This is to throw them off the track," he whispered as he stood straight again. "A little brotherly peck should do the trick."

"Yes, it should."

His gaze fell to her soft mouth for an instant. "Next time, I'll make sure I take you home last. Good night, angel."

"Good night."

He winked and walked to the car, whistling an off-key tune on the way. Natalie waved before she went into the house. She'd wanted Mack to kiss her again, but maybe he'd had enough kissing that afternoon. She hadn't. Not by a long shot. She didn't want to feel this way about Mack, but she couldn't help herself. She wondered how it would eventually work out between them, but it was too disturbing to torture herself like that. She cleaned her face, got into her gown and went to bed. And she dreamed of Mack all night long.

Chapter 6

The phone rang on the one morning during the week when Natalie could sleep late. It was Mack, and he sounded worried.

"It's Viv," he said at once, not bothering with a greeting. "I had to take her to the emergency room early this morning. She's got the flu and it's complicated with pneumonia. She refused to let me put her in the hospital, and I've got to fly out to Dallas this morning on business. My plane leaves in less than an hour and a half. The boys are off on a hunting trip. I hate to ask you, but can you come over and stay with her until I get home?"

"Of course I can," she replied. "How long are you going to be away?"

"With luck, I'll be back by midnight. If not, first thing tomorrow."

"I don't have to go in to the grocery store to work until tomorrow afternoon. I'll be glad to stay with her. Did the doctor give you prescriptions for her, and have you been to the pharmacy to pick up her medicine?"

"No," he said gruffly. "I'll have to do that —"

"I'll pick them up on my way over," she said. "You go ahead and catch your flight. I'll be there in thirty minutes if they have her prescriptions ready."

"They should be," he said. "I dropped them off before I brought her home. I'll phone and give them my credit card number, so they'll already be paid for."

"Thanks."

"Thank *you*," he added. "She feels pretty bad, so she shouldn't give you much trouble. Oh, and there's a little complication," he said irritably. "Whit's here."

"That should cheer her up," she reminded him.

"It will, as long as you don't look at him."

She laughed. "No problem there."

"I know you don't like him, but she won't believe it. If there was anybody else I could ask, I wouldn't bother you. I just don't like the idea of leaving her alone with him, even if she does have pneumonia."

"I don't mind. Honest. You be careful."

"The plane wouldn't dare crash," he chuckled. "I've got too much work to do."

"Keep that in mind. I'll see you when you get back."

"You be careful, too," he said. "And wear your raincoat. It's already sprinkling outside."

"I'll wear mine if you wear yours."

He chuckled again. "Okay. You win. I'll be home as soon as I can."

She said goodbye and hung up, rushing to get her bag packed so that she could get over to the ranch.

She walked into Viv's bedroom with a bag of medicine, a cold soft drink that she knew her friend liked and some cough drops.

Viv looked washed out and sick, but she managed a wan smile as Natalie approached the bed. Whit was sprawled in an armchair by the bed, looking out of sorts until he saw Natalie. His eyes ran over her trim figure in jeans and a button-up gray knit sweater with a jaunty gray and green scarf.

"Don't you look cute," he said with a smile.

Viv glared at him. So did Natalie.

"Why don't you make some coffee, Whit?" Viv asked angrily. "I could do with a cup."

He got out of the chair. "My pleasure. What do you take in yours, Nat?" he asked smoothly.

She turned and looked him right in the eye. "Nobody calls me Nat except Mack," she pointed out. "It isn't a nickname I tolerate from anyone else."

His cheekbones colored briefly. "Sorry," he said with a nervous laugh. "I'll just make that coffee. Be back as soon as I can."

Viv watched him go and then turned cold eyes on her friend. "You don't have to snap at him," she said curtly. "He was only being polite."

Natalie's eyebrows went up. "Was he?"

"Mack shouldn't have called you," she said tersely. "I'd have been just fine here with Whit."

Natalie felt uncomfortable and unwelcome. "He thought you needed nursing."

"He thought I needed a chaperone, you mean," she said angrily. "And I don't! Whit would manage just fine."

"All right, then," Natalie said with a forced smile. "I'll go home. There's your medicine and some cough drops. I guess Whit can pick up anything else you need. Sorry I bothered you."

She turned and walked to the door, almost in tears.

"Oh, Nat, don't go," Viv said miserably. "I'm sorry. You came all this way and even brought my medicine and I'm being horrible. Please come back."

Natalie had the door open. "You've got Whit. . . ."

"Come back," Viv pleaded.

Natalie closed the door and went to the armchair by the bed, but her eyes were wounded and faintly accusing as she sat.

"Listen, Whit doesn't like me," Natalie told Viv. "He's only flirting with me to make you jealous. Why can't you see that? What in the world could he see in me? I'm not pretty and I don't have any money."

"In other words, he wouldn't like me if I didn't have a wealthy background?" Viv asked pointedly.

"I said you were pretty, too," she replied. "I know you feel bad, Viv, but you're being unreasonable. We've been friends for a long time. I don't know you lately, you're so different."

Viv shifted against her pillows. "He talks about you, too, even when you aren't here."

"It isn't what you think," Natalie said, exasperated. "He's never said or done a thing out of line."

"He's very good-looking," Viv persisted.

"So are you," Natalie said. "But right now you're sick and you don't need to upset yourself like this. Mack asked me to take care of you, and that's what I'm going to do."

Viv studied her through fever-bright eyes. "Did you know that Glenna was going with him to Dallas?" she asked with undeniable venom.

Natalie forced herself not to react. "Why?" she asked carelessly.

"Beats me. I suppose she had something to do there, too. Anyway, I don't think he'll come back tonight. Do you?"

Natalie glared at her. "You really are a horror," she said through her teeth.

Viv flushed. "Yes, I guess I am," she agreed after a minute. "Mack said he wouldn't wish the boys and me on a wife. He said it wouldn't be fair to expect anyone to have to take us on, as well as him. I know Glenna wouldn't. She hates me."

"Your brother loves all three of you very much," Natalie said, disquieted by what Viv had said.

"Well, he's not my father. Bob and Charles are in their last two years of high school and then Bob wants to go into the Army. Charles wants to study law at Harvard. That will get them out of the way, and if I marry Whit, which I want to do,

Mack will have the house to himself." Her voice was terse and cool. She didn't quite meet Natalie's eyes. "Would you marry him, if he asked you?"

"That won't happen," Natalie said quietly.

"Are you sure of that?"

"Yes," came the soft reply. "I'm sure. Mack's self-sufficient and he doesn't want to be tied down. He's said often enough that marriage wasn't for him. Probably he and Glenna will go on together for years," she added, aching inside but not letting it show, "since they both like being uncommitted."

"Maybe you're right." Viv studied her friend curiously. "But he's very protective of you."

Natalie averted her eyes. "Why shouldn't he be? I'm like a second sister to him."

Vivian frowned. She didn't say anything. After a few seconds, she started coughing violently. Natalie handed her some tissues and helped her sit up with a pillow held to her chest to keep the pain at bay.

"Does that help?" Natalie asked gently when the spasm passed.

"Yes. Where did you learn that?" she asked.

"At the orphanage. One of the matrons

had pneumonia frequently. She taught me."

Viv dropped her eyes. Occasionally in her jealousy, she forgot how deprived Natalie's life had been until the Killains had come along. She knew how Nat felt about Mack, and she didn't understand her sudden need to hurt a woman who'd been nothing but kind to her ever since their friendship began. She was fiercely jealous that Whit seemed to prefer Natalie, which didn't help her burgeoning resentment toward her best friend. She was confused and envious and so miserable that she could hardly stand herself. She didn't know what she was going to do if Whit made a serious pass at Natalie. She was sure that she'd do something desperate, and that it would be the end of her long friendship with the other woman.

The hours dragged after that tense exchange. Natalie kept out of Vivian's bedroom as much as she could, busying herself with tidying up around the living room. Whit paused to flirt with her from time to time, but she managed to keep him away by reminding him of Viv's condition. He was getting on her nerves, and Viv was getting more unbearable by the minute.

When eight o'clock rolled around, it was all Natalie could do to keep from running for her life. Whit was still around, and for the past fifteen minutes, he'd been coming on to Natalie. She was on the verge of assault when Mack walked in unexpectedly.

He gave Natalie and Whit a speaking glance. They were standing close together and Whit was leaning over her. It looked as if he'd just broken up something, and his eye flashed angrily.

"Why don't you make another pot of coffee, Whit?" she asked quickly.

"As soon as I get back," he promised. "I need to run to the convenience store and get some cigarettes. I'm dying for a smoke."

"Okay," Natalie said.

Mack didn't say a word. With bridled fury, he watched the other man go. But when he shook off his raincoat, he smiled at Natalie as she took it and hung it on the rack for him.

"Did it rain all the way home?" she asked.

"Just about. How's Viv?"

"She's doing fine."

"Good." He caught her hand, pulled her into the study with him and closed the

131

door. "You can sit with me while I get these papers sorted. Then we'll go up and see Viv."

"Whit won't know where we are when he comes back."

He lifted an eyebrow. "It's my house."

"Point taken." She sat in the chair across from his big desk and watched him sort through a briefcase before he sat down with several stacks of papers and began putting them into files.

As she watched his hands, she thought back to the night Carl had been killed in the wreck . . .

It was a stormy night, with lightning flashes illuminating everything inside and outside the house where Natalie was living with her aunt, old Mrs. Barnes. It was her seventeenth birthday, and she was spending it alone, in tears, mourning the death of the only boy she'd ever loved. His death that night in a wreck, driving home from an out-of-town weekend fishing and camping trip with a cousin was announced on the late news. The cousin lived. Carl had died instantly, because he wasn't wearing a seat belt. The official cause of the one-car accident was driving too fast for conditions in a blinding rain. The car had veered off the highway at a high speed and crashed down a hill. One of her friends from school had called, almost distraught with grief, to tell Natalie before she had to find out from the news.

Carl Barkley had been the star quarterback of their high school football team. Natalie had been his date, and the envy of the girls in the senior class, for the Christmas dance. She was to be his date for the senior prom, as well. Handsome, blond, blue-eyed Carl, who was president of the Key Club, vice president of the student council, an honor student with a facility for physics that had gained him a place at MIT after graduation. Carl, dead at eighteen. Natalie couldn't stop crying.

At times like these, she ached for a family to console her. Old Mrs. Barnes, who'd given her a home during her junior year of high school and with whom she would live while she attended the local community college, was away for the weekend. She wasn't due back until the next morning. There was Vivian Killain, of course, her best friend. But Vivian had also been a friend of Carl, and she was too upset to drive. The only fight Natalie and Vivian had ever had was over Carl, because Vivian had started dating him first. Carl had only gone out with her once before he and Natalie ended up in English class together. It had been love at first sight for both of them, but Vivian only saw it as Natalie tempting her boyfriend away. It wasn't like that at all.

The thunder shook the whole house, and it wasn't until the rumble died down that Natalie heard someone knocking on the front door. Slipping a matching robe over a thin pink satin nightgown with spaghetti straps, she went to see who it was.

A tall, lean man in a raincoat and broad-brimmed Stetson stared at her.

"Vivian said your aunt was out of town and you were alone," Mack Killain said quietly, surveying her pale, drenched face. "I'm sorry about your boyfriend."

Natalie didn't say a word. She simply lifted her arms. He picked her up with a rough sound and kicked the door shut behind him. With her wet face buried in his throat, he carried her easily down the hall to the open door that was obviously her bedroom. He kicked that door shut, too, and sat her gently on the armchair beside the bed.

He took off his raincoat, draping it over the straight chair by the window, and placed his hat over it. He was wearing work clothes, she saw through her tears. He hadn't even stopped long enough to change out of his chaps and boots and spurs. His blue-checked long-sleeve shirt was open halfway down his chest, disclosing a feathery pattern of thick, black curling hair. His broad forehead showed the hat mark. A lock of raven-black straight hair fell over the thin black elastic of the eye patch over his left eye.

He stared at Natalie for a few seconds, taking in her swollen eyes and flushed cheeks, the paleness of the rest of her oval face.

"I didn't even get to say goodbye, Mack," she managed huskily.

"Who does?" he replied. He bent and lifted her so that he could drop down into the armchair with her in his lap. He curled her into his strong, warm body and held her while she struggled through a new round of tears. She clung to him, grateful for his presence.

She'd always been a little afraid of him, although she was careful not to let it show. She'd been the one who nursed him, over the objections of the orphanage, when he was gored in the face by one of his own bulls. His sister, Vivian, was no good at all with anyone who was hurt or sick — she simply went to pieces. And his brothers, Bob and Charles, were terrified of their big brother. Natalie had known that he stood to lose his sight in both eyes instead of just one, and she'd held him tight and told him over and over again that he mustn't give up. She'd stayed out of classes for a whole week while the doctors fought to save that one eye, and she hadn't left him day or night until he was able to go home.

Even then, she'd stopped by every day to check on him, having presumed that he'd have his family standing on its ear trying to keep him in bed for the pre-scribed amount of time. Sure enough, the boys had walked wide around him and Vivian just left him alone. Natalie had made sure that he did what the doctor told him to. It amused and amazed his siblings that he'd let her boss him around. Killain gave orders. He didn't take them from any-body — well, except from Natalie, when it suited him.

"We were going to the senior prom to-gether," she said huskily, wiping her eyes with the back of her hand. "This morning, I was deciding what sort of dress to wear and how I was going to fix my hair . . . and he's dead."

"People die, Nat," he said, his voice deep

and quiet and comforting at her ear. "But I'm sorry he did."

"You didn't know him, did you?"

"I'd spoken to him a time or two," he said with deliberate carelessness.

"He was so handsome," she said with a ragged sigh. "He was smart and brave and everybody loved him."

"Of course."

She shifted into a more comfortable position on his lap, and as she did, her hand accidentally slid under the fabric of his cotton shirt, to lie half buried in thick hair. Odd, how his powerful body tensed when it happened, she thought with confusion. She was aware of other things, too. He smelled of horses and soap and leather. His breath pulsed out just above her nose, and she could smell coffee on it. Her robe was open, and the tiny straps that held her gown up had slipped in her relaxed position. One of her breasts was pressed against Mack's chest, and she could feel warm muscle and prickly hair against it just above the nipple. Her body felt funny. She wanted to pull the gown away and press herself closer, so that his skin and hers would touch. She frowned, shocked by the longing she felt to be held hungrily by him.

She tensed a little. "You're still wearing

your work clothes," she said. Her voice sounded as odd as she felt. "Why?"

"We had a fence down and we didn't know it until the sheriff called and said we had cattle strung up and down the highway," he told her. "It's taken two hours to get them back in and fix the fence. That's why it took me so long to get here. Vivian had been calling me on my cell phone since dark, but I was out of the truck."

"Don't you have a flip phone as well as the one installed in your truck?" she wondered aloud.

He chuckled. "Sure. It's at home recharging."

She smiled drowsily. "Thank you for coming over. I'm sure you didn't feel like it after all that."

His broad shoulders lifted and fell. "I couldn't leave you here alone," he said simply. "And Vivian was in no sort of shape to come." His lean hand smoothed her wavy dark hair. "She thinks you cut her out with Carl, but that's just the way she is."

"I know." She sighed. "She's so pretty that she takes it for granted that the boys all want her. Most of them do, too."

"She's spoiled," he replied. "I was hard

138

on Bob and Charles, but I've made a lot of allowances for Viv, simply because she was the only girl in the family. Maybe that was a mistake."

"It's not a mistake to care for people," she pointed out.

"So they say." His fingers tangled in her soft hair. "Want something to drink?"

"No, thanks," she replied. Her fingers spread involuntarily in the thick hair over his breastbone, and his intake of breath was sharp and audible.

His body tensed again. She and Carl had kissed, but she'd been careful not to let things go very far. In fact, she hadn't felt any sort of strong physical attraction to the football star, which was strange, considering how much he meant to her. With Mack, she experienced sensations she'd never felt before. She felt hot and swollen in the most unusual places, and it puzzled her. The sudden tension she noticed in the man holding her puzzled her, as well. Mack didn't say a word, but she could feel his heartbeat increase, hear the rough sound of his breathing.

She let her face slide down his muscular arm, and her curious eyes met his good one. It was narrow and unblinking and vaguely intimidating. Even as she watched, his gaze went to where her robe was open and one of her breasts in its lace-trimmed satin lay soft and warm against his chest.

Involuntarily, she followed his intense scrutiny and saw what she hadn't realized before — the gown had slipped so far down that her nipple, hard and tight, was visibly pressing into the thick hair over his chest.

He looked into her stunned eyes, and the hand in her hair tightened. "Didn't you do this with your boyfriend?" he asked bluntly.

"No," she said shakily.

"Why not, if you loved him?" he persisted.

She frowned worriedly. It was becoming increasingly hard to think at all. "I didn't feel like this with him," she confessed in a whisper.

Mack's face changed. His hand in her hair arched her face to his and tugged it into the crook of his arm. He shifted, so that the bodice came completely away from one pert little breast, and his arm tightened, moving her skin sensuously against him.

She gasped. Her nails bit into his chest, and her lips parted in shock and delight. Involuntarily, she arched closer, so that her breast dragged roughly against his skin.

The hand in her hair began to hurt. His body tensed, and a faint shudder rippled through him.

His jaw clenched, and he fought his hunger. She realized that he wanted to feel her against him without the fabric between them, and it was what she wanted, as well. She forgot about wrong and right, about decency, about everything except the pleasure they were giving each other here, in the quiet room with the silence only broken by the sound of the rain outside the window and their breathing.

"I should be shot for doing this, and you should be shot for letting me," he said through his teeth. But even as he spoke, his free hand was stripping the robe and gown to her waist. His gaze fell to her naked breasts, and he shuddered again, violently, as his arm suddenly tightened and dragged her breasts against his hair-roughened chest in a feverish caress.

She moaned harshly. Her nails bit into the hard muscles of his upper arms as he crushed her against him and buried his face in the thick hair at her ear. He held her, rocked her, in an aching excess of desire.

Both arms were around her now. She slid

her arms around his neck and clung for dear life. She couldn't catch her breath at all. It was the most intense pleasure she'd ever known. She trembled with desire.

The embrace was fierce. They held each other in a tense silence that seemed to throb with need. Her fingers tangled in the hair at the nape of his strong neck, and her eyes closed as she lay against him, unafraid and unashamed of the growing intimacy of the embrace.

He could feel his body growing harder by the second. If he moved her any closer, she'd be able to feel it. He didn't want that. It was years too soon for the sort of intimacy they were leading up to. He could barely think at all, but the part of his brain that still worked was flashing with red warning lights. She was seventeen, just barely, and he was twenty-three. She wasn't old enough or experienced enough to know what was about to happen. He was. He couldn't take advantage of her like this. He had to pull away and stop while he still could.

Abruptly, he shot to his feet, taking her with him. He held her, swaying on her feet, just in front of him. For one long, tense moment, his gaze went to her taut, bare breasts and his face seemed to clench.

Then he pulled the straps up and replaced them on her shoulders, easing the robe into place. He tied it with swift, sharp movements of his big hands.

She stared at him, too overwhelmed by the intimacy and its abrupt end to think clearly. "Why did you stop?" she asked softly. "Did I do something wrong?"

Her pale green eyes made him ache as they searched his face. He caught her by the waist and took a slow, deliberate breath before he spoke. "Didn't they teach sex education at the orphanage?" he asked bluntly.

Her face flamed scarlet. Her eyes, like saucers, seemed to widen endlessly.

He shook his head. She was so deliciously naïve. He felt a generation apart from her instead of only six years. "A man can't take much of that without doing something about it, Nat," he said gently. "Looking isn't enough."

She was embarrassed, but she didn't drop her eyes. "I never could have done that with Carl," she said, feeling vaguely guilty about it. "I enjoyed kissing him, but I never wanted him to do anything else. I didn't like it when he tried to."

He ached to his boots. His hands contracted on her shoulders. "You're only

143

seventeen," he reminded her. "I know Carl was special to you, but you aren't really old enough for a physical relationship with anyone."

"My mother was just eighteen when she had me," she pointed out.

"This is a different world than hers," he countered. "And even for an innocent woman, you're remarkably backward."

"Weren't you, at my age?" she asked in a driven tone.

He pursed his lips and studied her face. "At your age, I'd already had my first woman. She was two years my senior and pretty experienced for a place like Medicine Ridge. She taught me."

She felt her heartbeat racing madly in her chest. She hadn't expected him to be innocent, but it was shocking to have him speak about it so bluntly.

His lean fingers brushed over her cheek. "And when you're old enough," he said in a strange, caressing tone, "I'll teach you."

Those shocking words from the past resonated in her mind as she looked at him in the dimly lit study. *I'll teach you. I'll teach you.*

While she was reliving the past, he'd gotten out of his chair and moved around the desk. He was propped against it, his jacket and tie off, his arms folded, watching her.

"Oh," she said, blinking. "Sorry. I was lost in thought. Literally." She laughed softly.

He didn't smile. "Come here, Nat."

She measured the distance to the door and then laughed inwardly at her cowardice. She'd adored this man for so many years that she couldn't imagine letting anyone else touch her, ever. Besides, she assured herself, he had Glenna to satisfy those infrequent urges he'd once spoken of so bluntly. He wanted to talk without being overheard by Whit in case he came back unexpectedly, that was why he wanted her closer.

With a self-mocking smile she came to a stop less than arm's length away and looked at him.

He let his gaze encompass her, from her flat moccasins to the thrust of her breasts against the thin sweater. The top two buttons were undone, hinting at the cleavage below.

"I shouldn't leave Viv alone too long," she began.

He ignored the hint. His fingers spread along her cheek and his gaze dropped to her soft mouth. "Viv can wait," he replied quietly. His thumb abruptly moved roughly across her lips, sensitizing them in a shock of desire.

His good eye narrowed. "Go and lock the door," he said in a tone he hadn't used with her since the night Carl had died.

She wasn't going to be dictated to, she told herself. Even Mack wasn't going to be allowed to tell her what to do!

So it came as a surprise that she closed the door and locked it, her back to him. She was almost shaking with desire. She leaned her hot forehead against the cold wood of the door, hearing the jerk of her breath in her throat.

She didn't hear him approach, because the thick carpet muffled the sound of his footsteps. But she felt him at her back, felt the heat of his powerful body as both arms went past her to the door. He moved deliberately close, so that his body made contact with hers from her shoulders to her thighs. The contours of his body changed instantly, and she knew, even in her innocence, that what they shared was something rare.

"And now you know why I put you away so quickly that night, don't you?" he asked quietly.

She swallowed, her body involuntarily responding to his need by arching toward him. "Yes. I do now."

His hands slid to her flat belly and pulled her closer to him.

"You felt this way all those years ago?" she said, realizing.

"Yes." His hands smoothed to her rib cage and hesitated. "I accumulated a fair share of experience when I was younger," he continued. "But in recent years, sex has become a more serious matter to me. I've gone hungry. You were innocent and curious, and I almost lost control with you. I didn't feel comfortable letting you see how tempted I was — especially under the circumstances."

"I'm still innocent," she reminded him without turning.

"And just as curious," he concluded for her. His hands flattened over her rib cage and became possessive. "But tonight, I'm going to satisfy your curiosity. Completely." And he turned her around.

Chapter 7

Natalie caught her breath at the look on Mack's face. The naked hunger in that one beautiful dark eye was almost frightening.

His big, lean hands framed her face as he searched her eyes. "Don't be afraid of me," he said softly. "I'd cut off my arm before I'd ever hurt you."

"I know that." She studied him worriedly. "But I can't —"

His lips caught the words and stopped them. She felt his hands drop to her throat and then to her shoulders, smoothing up and down the skin left bare by her short-sleeve sweater. He was slow and tender and sensual. It was like a dance in slow motion, a poem, a symphony.

The door was hard at her back as he moved closer, trapping her between his body and the wood. One long leg inserted itself confidently between both of hers with a lazy movement that was as arousing as the kiss they were sharing.

She gasped, and his mouth lifted away. He looked at her, breathing a little jerkily.

"This is perfectly natural," he said quietly. "Don't fight it."

Her eyes were wild and a little frightened by the overwhelming desire she felt. "You went away . . . with Glenna," she whispered.

"She went on the plane," he corrected. "She didn't go with me." His mouth traced her eyelids and closed them. His hands were under her arms, lifting her closer. They moved slowly, gently, onto her breasts and caressed them with lazy delight.

She felt her legs go weak underneath her. It was unlike any other time she'd been in his arms. He handled her as if she belonged to him, as if she were precious to him, cherished by him.

Her eyes opened when he lifted his head, and they were full of wonder, wide with breathless hunger and delight. Her heart was in them.

He searched them quietly, and a faint smile touched his hard mouth. "I've waited years for that expression," he said under his breath. "Years."

He bent again, and this time her arms lifted slowly around his neck, cradling his head as his mouth covered her parted lips. They clung to each other, letting the kiss build, feeling its power. She moaned when it became fierce and hungry, but she didn't try to get away. Involuntarily, her body pressed hard against his.

She felt him shiver. He pushed down, his hands lifting her suddenly into the hard thrust of him and holding her there with a slow, sensual rhythm that made her tremble and gasp into his mouth.

"Sweetheart!" he whispered roughly.

The kiss grew harder. She felt him move and lift her clear off the floor in his arms. He walked to the sofa and spread her lengthwise on the leather, easing his body down to cover hers in a silence that was heated and tense.

He was fiercely aroused, and she wanted him at that moment more than she'd ever wanted anything in her life. She followed where he led, even when she felt him shifting her so that his lean hips were pressed squarely against hers, between her legs, in an intimacy that was suddenly urgent and feverish with dark pleasure. She couldn't have pushed him away if her survival had depended on it. Presumably he felt the same, because his arms held her relentlessly as he began to move against her.

She shuddered with the riptide of pleasure the movement produced, and her eyes flew open, locking with his dark, passionate gaze as he lifted his head to look at her.

With his hands at her head, taking most of his weight, he moved deliberately, watching her as she lifted to meet him and gasped at the sensations the contact produced. Her nails bit into his hard arms, but she wasn't fighting. She was melting into the leather, flying up into the sky, burning, burning!

The intimacy became so torturous, so fierce, that it was almost too late to draw back when he realized what was happening to them. His hands caught her hips in a bruising clasp and he pulled her over him, holding her still, with her cheek on his pounding chest as he fought to breathe and stop all at the same time.

"No!" She choked, trying to return to the intimacy of their former embrace.

His hands forced her to be still. His breath at her forehead was hot and shaky, audible in the stillness of the study. "Don't," he bit off. "Don't move. For God's sake, don't!"

Her mouth pressed into the cotton of his shirt, hot and hungry. "I want to," she choked.

"God, don't you think I want to?" he demanded huskily. His hands hurt in their fight to keep her still. "I want you to the point of madness. But not like this, Natalie!"

Belatedly, she realized that he was trying to save her from her own hunger for him. It wasn't a thought she cherished at the moment, when her whole body was burning with a passion she'd never felt before. But slowly, the trembling eased and she began to breathe normally, if a little fast.

His hands smoothed over her hair, bunching it at her nape as he held her cheek to his chest.

"Why?" she whispered miserably when she was able to speak.

"Because I can't marry you," he explained. "And because you can't live with sleeping with me if I don't."

All her dreams vanished in a haze. As the room came into focus across his broad chest, she realized just how far gone they were and how intimate their position on the sofa had become. If he hadn't stopped, they'd be lovers already. She hadn't even protested. But he'd had the presence of mind to stop.

So much for her willpower and her principles, she thought sadly. It seemed that her body had a will of its own, and it was much stronger than her mind.

Tears poured from her eyes, and she didn't even notice until she felt his shirt become damp under her cheek.

His hand laced into her hair and soothed her scalp. "If I thought it would help matters, I'd cry, too," he murmured dryly.

She hit his shoulder with her fist. "How could you do that to me?" she demanded.

"How could you do it to me?" he shot back. "You know how I feel about commitment. I've said so often enough."

"You started it," she raged.

He sighed. "Yes, I did," he admitted after a minute. "This is all I've been able to think about since we went nightclubbing," he confessed. "That was probably the most misguided thing I've done in recent years. It's hard to put out a brushfire once it's started. Or didn't you notice?"

She moved experimentally and felt him help her move away to a healthy distance, lying beside him on the long leather couch with her cheek on his shoulder. She looked at him quietly, curiously. His face was a little flushed, and his mouth was swollen from the hard, hungry kisses they'd shared. His shirt was open at the throat. His hair was disheveled. He looked as though he'd been making love, and probably so did she. She didn't really mind. He looked sensual like that.

"You'd better leave town," he suggested with a wry smile. "You just went on the endangered list."

Her fingers spread on his shirt, but he caught and stilled them. "Stop that. I'm barely a step away from ravishment."

"How exciting," she murmured.

"You wouldn't think so for the first few minutes," he murmured skeptically. "And you wouldn't be able to live with your conscience even if you did enjoy it eventually."

She grimaced. "I guess not. I'm not really cut out for passionate affairs."

"And I'm not cut out for happily ever after," he said without looking at her.

"Because of your family?" she asked.

He drew in a long breath. She felt his chest rise and fall under her hand. "We could make a list. It wouldn't change anything." He looked at her rapt, soft face, and his hardened. "Despite everything," he whispered huskily, "I would give everything I own to have you, just once."

She managed a faint smile. "Maybe you'd be disappointed."

He traced her mouth with a lazy finger. "Maybe you would, too."

"So it's just as well, isn't it?"

"That's what my mind says," he agreed.

She nuzzled against his shoulder and closed her eyes. "Isn't there a poem about hopeless attraction?"

"Hundreds," he said.

She felt his hand smoothing her hair, almost in a comforting gesture. She smiled. "That feels nice."

"You feel nice, lying against me like this," he whispered. He bent and kissed her closed eyelids with breathless tenderness. "It was like this, the night of the wreck," he added in a hushed tone. "I held you and comforted you, and wanted you until I ached."

"But I was seventeen."

"But you were seventeen." He pressed a kiss on her forehead and put her aside so that he could get to his feet. "You haven't changed much," he added as he helped her up.

"I'm older," she pointed out.

He laughed, and it had a hollow sound. "If you were a modern woman, we'd have fewer problems."

"But I'm not modern," she replied sadly. "And that says it all."

A door opened and shut, and he glanced toward the closed door of the study.

"That'll be Romeo, I reckon," he drawled with a glittery look at Natalie. "I don't like the way he hangs around you."

"He likes me," she said carelessly. "I like him, too. What's wrong with that?"

"He belongs to Vivian," he returned, and he didn't smile.

She searched his hard face. "You can't own people."

The eyebrow that wasn't under the string of the eye patch lifted sardonically. "She won't thank you for making a play for him."

She ached all over with frustration and misery, and she hated him for arousing her and pushing her away at the same time. It wasn't logical, but then, she wasn't thinking clearly. She didn't mean what she said next, but she was so angry she couldn't help herself. "What would you care if I did? You don't like him. Maybe it would open her eyes."

"Don't do it," he warned in a low, threatening tone.

"Or you'll do what?" she challenged icily.

He didn't answer. They were enemies in the blink of an eye. He was furious, and it showed. He went to the door and opened it with a jerk, waiting for her to leave.

She hesitated, but only for an instant. If that was the way he wanted it, all right! She went out the door without looking at him, without speaking, without knowing that she'd just altered the whole pattern of her life.

Mack closed the door sharply behind her, and she grimaced before she went to the kitchen to see if Whit was there. He was. He'd just made coffee, in one of the expensive modern coffee machines that did it in seconds. He'd poured two cups, one for himself and one for Vivian.

"Where's the tray?" he asked, looking around.

"I haven't got a clue," she admitted. She looked in cupboards, but she couldn't find one.

"Never mind," he said. "I take mine black and she takes hers with cream. I can carry both cups if you'll bring the cream, and we'll forget the tray."

"Okay," she said.

He was gazing at her with an experienced eye, and it suddenly occurred to her that she must look pretty disheveled. She thought about taking a minute to repair her makeup before she went upstairs, but Whit was already out the door.

She followed him up the staircase and into Vivian's room. It hadn't dawned on her, either, that Whit had been out in the wind and his hair was disheveled. When the two of them entered the room, Vivian put together Natalie's swollen mouth and mussed hair and Whit's mussed hair and came up with infidelity.

"Go home," she told Natalie in a vicious tone. "Go right now and don't ever come back!"

"Viv! What's wrong?" she asked.

"As if you don't know!"

Whit didn't say anything, but he had a very strange look in his eyes. "You'd better go," he said gently. "I'll look after Viv."

Natalie looked at Vivian, but she turned her face away and refused to say another word. With resignation and bitter sadness, Natalie put down the cream and left the room.

Nobody was around when she went out the front door. She'd made a clean sweep tonight. Mack and Vivian were both furious at her over Whit when she hadn't meant to cause trouble. She hoped it would all blow over.

For the moment, all she could think about was the close call she'd had in Mack's arms on the sofa, and she wished with all her heart that things had been different between them. For better or worse, she loved him with her whole heart. But he had nothing to offer her.

She went home and fell, exhausted, into bed.

Whit was left alone with Vivian, who was in tears. "You were making love to her!" she accused, her blue eyes shooting sparks at him. "My boyfriend and my best friend! How could you?"

He hesitated before he spoke, with both hands in his pockets. He'd seen Vivian as a nice, biddable little source of gambling money and light lovemaking. But she'd become jealous and possessive of him, and he was getting tired of it. There were other women.

"So what?" he asked, not denying her charge. "She's not as pretty or rich as you are, but she's sweet and she doesn't question every move I make."

Vivian stared at him, almost purple with rage and frustration and hurt pride. "Then go with her," she spat at him. "Get out. And don't come back!"

"That," he replied, "will actually be a pleasure. You're no man's idea of the perfect woman, Viv. In fact, you're a spoiled

little rich girl who wants to own people.
It's not worth it."

"Worth what?" she choked.

He looked at her with world-weary cyni-
cism and contempt. "I like to gamble. You
had money. We made a handsome couple.
I thought we'd be a match made in heaven.
But there are other rich girls, honey."

He laughed mockingly and walked out,
closing the door behind him. Vivian went
wild, throwing things and weeping horribly
until Mack came into the room minutes
later and helped her off the floor and into
bed.

"What in God's name is wrong with
you?" he demanded, surveying the destruc-
tion of her bedroom.

"Whit and Natalie," she choked. "They
were . . . making love. . . . Whit said she
was everything I'm not." Sobs choked the
words for several seconds while her brother
stood by the bed, frozen. "Oh, I hate them
so. I hate them both! My boyfriend and my
best friend! How could they do this to
me?"

"How do you know they were making
love?" he asked in a hollow tone.

"I saw them," she lied viciously. "And
Whit admitted it. He even laughed about
it!"

Mack's face became a mask. He drew the covers over Vivian with a strange, frightening silence.

Vivian wasn't making connections. She was just short of hysteria. "They won't come here again. I told them not to. I'm through with them!"

"Yes." His voice sounded strained. "Try to calm down. You'll make yourself sicker."

"If either of them call," Vivian added coldly, "I won't speak to them."

"Don't worry about that," he told her. "I'll handle it."

"I already handled it," she shot back. "And don't tell Bob and Charles. Nobody else needs to know!"

"All right, Viv. Try to get some sleep. I'll have Sadie come in tomorrow and clean up in here."

"Thanks, Mack," she managed through her tears. "You really are a dear."

He didn't answer her. He went out and closed the door quietly, and the life seemed to drain out of him. Natalie, with Vivian's boyfriend. He'd told her not to flirt with the man, and she'd been angry with him. Was that why? Did it explain why she'd go from his arms into another man's in less than ten minutes?

Well, if her idea was to make him

jealous, it had failed. He had nothing but contempt for her. Like Vivian, he didn't want her in the house, in his life. He went downstairs to his study and immersed himself in paperwork, trying not to see that long leather couch where they'd lain together in the sweetest interlude of his life.

Maybe it was just as well. He couldn't marry her. There were too many strikes against them. But he didn't like the idea of her with that gambler. Or any other man . . .

He cursed his hateful memory and put the pencil down. Natalie ran like a golden thread through so much of his life. In recent years, she'd been involved in just about everything that went on at the ranch. She rode with him and Vivian, she came to parties, barbecues, cattle sales. She was always around. Now he wouldn't see her come running up the steps, laughing in that unaffected way she had. She wouldn't flirt with him, chide him, lecture him. He was going to be alone.

He got up and went to the liquor cabinet. He seldom drank, but he kept a bottle of aged Scotch whiskey for guests. He poured himself a shot and threw it down, enjoying the hot sting of it as it washed down his throat. He couldn't remember a time when he'd felt so powerless. He looked at the bottle and carried it to the desk. As an afterthought, he locked the door.

Vivian couldn't sleep. She got up and washed her face, careful of the broken objects she'd dashed against walls in her rage. She kept remembering Mack's face when she'd told him about Natalie and Whit. She'd never seen such an expression.

It bothered her enough to go looking for him. He wasn't in his room or anywhere upstairs. Walking slowly, because it was difficult to walk and breathe at the same time despite the antibiotic, she made it to the door of his study. She tried to open the door, but it was locked. Mack never locked the door.

She hesitated, but only for a moment. She combined the look on his face with his strange behavior and the way he'd held Natalie when they'd danced at the nightclub, and with trembling hands she went to the intercom panel and called the foreman.

"I want you to come up here right now," she said after identifying herself. "Haven't we got a man who does locksmithing part-time?"

"Yes, ma'am," he said.

"Bring him, too. And hurry!"

"Yes, ma'am!"

She sat down in the hall chair, biting her lip. It had been a lie that she'd seen Natalie and Whit together, but they both looked as if they'd been kissing. And Whit hadn't denied it. But if Mack was in love with Natalie, which was becoming a disturbing possibility, she might have caused a disaster. Despite Glenna's persistence, Mack had never behaved as if he couldn't live without her. But the way he watched Natalie, the way he'd held her on the dance floor, the way his gaze followed her . . . oh, God, let those men hurry!

It seemed like an eternity before the doorbell sounded. She went as quickly as she could to answer it.

"I want you to unlock this door," she told the man beside the foreman.

"Can't you use the key?" he asked, clearly hesitant.

"I don't have the key. Mack does, and he's locked himself in there." She wrapped her arms over her thick bathrobe. "Please," she said in an uncharacteristic request for help. Gone was the autocratic manner. "There's been some . . . some trouble. He's in there. He won't answer me."

Without a word, the locksmith took out

his leather packet of tools and went to work. In short order, he had the door unlocked.

"Wait," she said when they started to open it. "Wait here. I'll call you if I need you." She didn't want to expose her brother to gossip if there was no need.

She went inside and closed the door. The sight that met her eyes was staggering. It made her shiver with guilt. Mack was lying facedown on the desk, a nearly empty whiskey bottle overturned at his hand. Mack never drank to excess; the memory of his father's alcoholism stopped him.

She went to the door and opened it just a crack. "He's just asleep. Thank you for your trouble. You can go."

"Are you sure, Miss Killain?" the foreman asked.

"Yes," she said confidently. "I'm sure."

"Then, good night. We'll come back if you need us."

Both men left. Vivian curled up in the big chair beside the desk and sat there all night with her brother. For the first time in her life, she realized how self-absorbed she'd become.

In the morning, very early, he woke up. He sat, dizzy, and scowled when he saw his sister curled in her robe in the big chair by the desk. He swept back his hair and surveyed the remains of the whiskey.

"Viv?" he called roughly. "What the hell do you think you're doing down here?"

She opened her eyes, still very sick. "I was worried about you," she said. "You never drink."

He held his head. "I never will again, I can promise you," he said wryly.

She uncurled and got slowly to her feet. "Are you all right?"

His shoulder moved jerkily. "I'm fine. How about you?"

She managed a smile. "I'll get by."

His face locked up tight. "We were both bad judges of character," he said.

"About what I said last night," she began earnestly. "I ought to tell you —"

He held up a big hand, and his face was hard with distaste. "They deserve each other," he said flatly. "You know I go around with Glenna," he added. "I don't want a long-term relationship, least of all with a penniless, fickle, two-timing orphan!"

She felt two inches high. She did blame Natalie, but she had a terrible feeling that Mack would never recover. It would take her a while to get over Whit's betrayal, as well. But she felt guilty and ashamed for making matters worse.

"Maybe they couldn't help it," she said heavily.

"Maybe they didn't want to," he returned. He got to his feet. "And that's all I'll ever say on the matter. I don't want to hear her name mentioned in this house ever again."

"All right, Mack."

He looked at the whiskey bottle with cold distaste before he dropped it into the trash can by the desk.

"Let's get you back upstairs," he told Viv with a smile. "I'm supposed to be taking care of you."

She slid her arm around his waist. "You're my brother. I love you."

He kissed her forehead and hugged her close. "Thanks."

She shrugged. "We're Killains. We're survivors."

"You bet we are. Come on."

He put her back to bed and went to see about the animals in the barn. He didn't think about the night before. And when Bob and Charles came home, nothing of what had happened was mentioned. But Vivian managed to get them alone long enough to warn them not to talk about

Natalie at all in front of Mack.

"Why not?" Bob wanted to know, puzzled. "She's like family."

"Sure she is," Charles emphasized. "We all love her."

Vivian couldn't meet their eyes. "It's a long story. She's done something to hurt me and Mack. We don't want to talk about it, okay?"

They were reluctant, but she persuaded them. If she could only persuade her conscience that she was the wronged party. She couldn't forget what Whit had said to her. Natalie had been her only best friend for years. Was it realistic that Natalie would make a play for her boyfriend? She had for Carl, all those years ago, Vivian thought bitterly, and then she remembered that Carl had only been dating Natalie for a bet. She'd known, and she hadn't told Natalie because she was jealous of her relationship with Carl. In hindsight, she began to see how painfully unfair she'd been. Her whole life had been one of pampered security. Natalie hadn't had the advantages Vivian had, but she'd never been envious or jealous of Vivian. Remembering that made Vivian feel even more guilty. But it was too late to undo the damage. If Whit was telling the truth, everyone would know it soon, because Natalie would be seen going around with him. Then, Vivian told herself, she'd be vindicated.

But it didn't happen. In fact, Whit was seen with the daughter of a local contractor who had plenty of money and liked to gamble. They were the talk of the town, so soon after Whit's visible break with Vivian.

As for Natalie, she'd gone home the night of the uproar and, surprisingly, slept all night and most of the morning after she cried herself to sleep. She barely made it to the grocery store in time to work her shift. She was grateful for the job, because it took her mind off the painful argument with Mack and the vicious tongue-lashing Vivian had given her. For the first time in years, she really did feel like an orphan. She was worried about how her exams would be graded, as well, and about graduation. It seemed that the weight of the world had fallen on her over the weekend. Worst of all, of course, was Mack's anger. Perhaps she'd provoked it, but the pain was terrible.

Chapter 8

Natalie received her grades from the registrar the following week, and she laughed out loud with relief when she saw that she'd passed all her subjects. She would graduate, after all.

But as her classmates placed their orders for tickets to the baccalaureate service and the graduation exercises, Natalie realized with a start that she had no one to get tickets for. None of the Killains were speaking to her, and she had no family. She would have nobody to watch her graduate.

It was a painful realization. She went through the rehearsals and picked up her cap and gown, but without much enthusiasm. No one would have known from her bright exterior that she was unhappy. Even at work, she pretended that she was on top of the world.

She saw Dave Markham briefly before her big day. They hadn't had much contact since her student teaching stint had been over, and she'd missed his pleasant company.

"I hear through the grapevine that you're graduating," he told her, tongue in cheek, as he waited at the grocery store for her to check out his groceries.

She grinned. "So they say. It's really a relief. I wondered during exams if I was going to pass everything."

"Everyone goes through that," he assured her. "Finals in your senior year are enough to cause a nervous breakdown." He studied her quietly as she bent over the computer keyboard after she'd scanned his purchases into the machine. "There's another rumor going around."

She stopped, her head lifting. "Which is?"

He grimaced. "That you've had a split with the Killains," he continued. "I didn't believe it, though. You and Vivian have been friends for years."

"Sadly," she said, "it's true." She drew in a long breath as she gave him his total, then waited for him to count out the amount and give it to her.

He waited while she finalized the transaction before he spoke again, taking the sales slip automatically. "What happened? Can you tell me?"

She called for one of the grocery boys to come and help her bag his purchases before she turned to him. "I'd rather not,

Dave," she said honestly. "It hurts to talk about it."

"That's why it hurts, because you haven't opened up." His eyes narrowed. "I hear Whit Moore's going around with a new girl and Vivian's quit taking classes at the vocational school."

That was news. "Did she?" She couldn't really blame her former best friend for that decision, of course. It wouldn't have been easy for her to go back into one of Whit's classes after they'd broken up in such a terrible way. She wondered if he'd ever been honest with Vivian about what had happened that night and decided that he probably hadn't. It was a major misunderstanding that might never be cleared up, and Natalie missed not only her former friend, but the boys, as well. She missed Mack most of all. She supposed that he'd heard all about it from Vivian. She'd hoped that he wouldn't believe his sister, but that was a forlorn hope. Natalie had never, in her acquaintance with the other girl, known her to tell Mack a deliberate lie.

"Mrs. Ringgold asks about you all the time," Dave added, trying to cheer her up. "She said she hopes you'll come and teach at our school in the fall, if there's an opening. So do I. I miss having you to talk to."

She remembered his hopeless love and smiled with fellow feeling. "Maybe I'll do just that," she said.

The bag boy came to sack his groceries, another customer pushed a cart up behind him, and the brief conversation was over. He left with a promise to call her and she went back to work, trying to put what she'd learned out of her mind. She wished Mack would call, at least, to give her a chance to explain the misunderstanding. But he didn't. And after Vivian's fierce hostility, she was nervous about phoning the house at all. She hoped that things would work themselves out, if she was patient.

Late afternoon on the Thursday before baccalaureate exercises Friday night, she walked out of the bank after depositing her paycheck and ran right into Mack Killain.

It was the first time she'd seen him since the day she'd had the falling out with Vivian. He moved away from her, and the look he gave her was so contemptuous, so full of distaste, that she felt dirty. That was when she realized that Vivian must have told Mack what she thought Natalie and

Whit had done. It was painfully obvious that Mack wasn't going to listen to an excuse. She'd never imagined that he would look at her like that. The pain went all the way to her soul.

"How could you do that to Vivian, to your best friend?" he asked coldly.

"Do . . . what?" she faltered.

"You know what!" he thundered. "You two-timing, lying, cheating little flirt. He must be crazy. No man in his right mind would look twice at you."

Her mouth fell open. Her heart raced. Her mouth was dry as cotton. "Mack . . ."

"You had us all fooled," he continued, raising his voice and not minding who heard. Several people did. "Vivian trusted you! And while she was in bed with pneumonia, you were making out with the man she loved!"

Natalie wanted to go through the sidewalk. Her eyes brimmed over with tears. "I didn't!" she tried to defend herself, almost choking on the words.

"There's no use denying it. Vivian saw you," he said with magnificent contempt. "She told me."

It was a lie, but he believed it. Maybe he wanted to believe it. He'd said that they had no future together, and this would make the perfect excuse for him to push her out of his life. Nothing she said was going to make any difference. He simply did not want her, and he was making it clear.

She'd thought the pain was bad before. Now it was unbearable.

"All of us trusted you, made you part of our family. And this is how you repaid us, by betraying Vivian, who never did anything to hurt you." His tone was vicious, furious. "Not only that, Natalie, you didn't even try to apologize for it."

She lifted her face defiantly. "I have nothing to apologize for," she said in a husky, hoarse tone.

"Then we have nothing to say to each other, ever again," he replied harshly.

"Mack, if you'd just let me try to explain," she said, hoping for a miracle. "Calm down and talk to me."

"I am calm," he said in an icy tone. "What did you expect, anyway? A proposal of marriage?" He laughed bitterly. "You know where I stand on that issue. And even if I were in the mood for it, it wouldn't be with a woman who'd sell me out the minute the ring was on her finger. You went to him afterward," he gritted, "and you as much as told me you were

175

going to. But if you think I'm jealous, honey, you're dead wrong. You were Vivian's friend, but I never wanted you hanging around my house. I tolerated you for Vivian's sake."

"I see." Her face was white and she was aware of pitying, embarrassed looks around her, because he was eloquent.

He hardened his heart, bristling with wounded pride as he looked at her, furious at his own weakness. Well, never again. "Which reminds me, Natalie," he added coldly, "I suppose it goes without saying that you're not welcome at the ranch anymore."

She lifted her eyes to his hard face and nodded slowly. "Yes, Mack," she said in a subdued tone. "It does go without saying."

Her heart was breaking. She turned away from that accusing, contemptuous gaze and walked briskly down the street to get away from him. She didn't know how she was going to bear this latest outrage of Vivian's. It had cost her Mack, whom she loved more than her own life. And he hated her. He hated her!

The bystanders were still staring at Mack when she was out of sight, but he didn't say a word. He stalked into the bank, noticing that people almost fell over trying to get out of his way. He was furious. After going right out of his arms into Whit's, she'd had the gall to try and deny it, even when Vivian had seen her with Whit! He would never trust his instincts about women again, he decided. If he could be fooled that easily, for that long, he was safer going around with Glenna. She might not be virtuous, but at least she was loyal — in her fashion.

Natalie went home with her heart around her knees. She made supper but couldn't eat it. She'd assumed that Mack was making assumptions. It hadn't occurred to her that Vivian would tell such a lie, or that Mack would believe it. But she'd helped things along by making those remarks to Mack in frustration when he'd put her out of the office after their tempestuous interlude. She hadn't wanted Whit, ever. But nobody would believe that now. She'd lost not only Mack, but the only family she'd known for years. She went to bed and lay awake most of the night, wretched and alone.

She wondered how she could go on living in the same town with the Killains and see Mack and Vivian and the boys week after week. Did Bob and Charles hate her, too? Was it a wholesale contempt?

Vivian had lied. That a woman she'd considered her best friend could treat her so callously hurt tremendously. Perhaps she was doomed to a life without affection. God knew that her aunt, old Mrs. Barnes, had only brought her from the orphanage to be a housekeeper and part-time nurse until the old lady died. No one had ever loved her. She'd wanted Mack to. She'd even thought at odd moments that he did, somehow. But the hatred in his eyes was damning. If he'd loved her, he'd have at least given her the benefit of the doubt.

But he hadn't. He'd believed Vivian without hesitation. So all her dreams of love eternal had gone up in smoke. There was nothing left except to make a decision about what she was going to do with the rest of her life. She knew immediately that she couldn't stay in Medicine Ridge. She would have to leave. Next week, after graduation, she was going to talk to one of her instructors who'd told her she knew of a job opening in a Dallas school where a relative was principal. Dallas sounded like a nice place to live.

Natalie marched in with her class to the baccalaureate service, trying not to notice how many of her classmates' whole families had come to see them in their caps and gowns. It was a brief service, held in the college chapel with a guest speaker who was some sort of well-known political figure. Natalie barely heard what went on around her because she was so heartbroken.

When the service was over, she greeted classmates she knew and drove herself home. The next morning, she got up early to go to the college with her gown for the graduation exercises. She felt very proud of her accomplishment as she marched into the chapel along with her class and waited for her name to be called, for her diploma to be handed out. It would have been one of the best days of her life, if the Killains hadn't been angry with her. As it was, she went through the motions like a zombie, smiling, looking happy for the cameras. But inside, she was so miserable that she only wanted to be alone. The minute the service was over, she went to look for the teacher who'd offered to help her get the Dallas job. And she told her she was interested.

The Killains were somber at the dinner table on Sunday. It was the first time in days they'd all been together, with the boys home, as well. It was more like a wake than a meal.

"Natalie graduated yesterday," Bob said coolly, glaring at Mack and Vivian, who wouldn't look at him. "My friend Gig's sister was in her class. She said that Natalie didn't have one single person of her own in the crowd for baccalaureate or graduation. Viv?"

Vivian had burst into tears. She pushed away from the table and went upstairs as fast as her healing lungs would allow.

Mack threw down his napkin, leaving his supper untouched, and stalked out of the room, as grim as death itself.

Bob looked at his brother and grimaced. "I guess I should have kept my mouth shut."

"I don't see why," Charles replied irritably. "Natalie belongs to us, to all of us. But the two of them behave as if she's at the top of the FBI's most-wanted list. It's that damned Whit, you mark my words. He did something or said something that caused this. He's going around with old Murcheson's daughter now, and she's grubstaking his gambling habit. Everybody knows it. He even said that our sister was only a means to an end, so if Natalie was the cause of that breakup, good for her!

She saved Viv from something a lot worse than pneumonia. Not that anybody but us cares, I guess," he muttered as he attacked his steak.

In the hall, Mack overheard and scowled. He'd thought Whit had left Vivian for Natalie, so why was he going around with the Murcheson girl? First Natalie's impassioned denial, now Viv's hysterical retreat. Something was wrong here.

He followed Vivian upstairs to her room. She was sitting in the chair by her bed, tears rolling down her pale cheeks. He sank down on the bed facing her.

"Why don't you tell me why you're crying, Viv," he invited gently.

She wiped at her red eyes with a tissue to catch the tears. "I lied," she whispered.

His whole body stiffened. "I beg your pardon?"

"I mean, Natalie was pretty disheveled and Whit's hair was ruffled. They looked like they'd been making out," she said defensively. "I didn't actually see them, though. But there was nobody else in the house except the two of them and they were down there for almost an hour." Her face hardened as she said it, so she missed the sudden pallor of her brother's face.

"I was down there," he snapped. "Whit went out to get cigarettes. He'd just come back and made coffee when he and Natalie went up to your room."

She gaped at him. Her jaw fell. Horror claimed her face. "Oh, no," she whispered. "Oh, dear God, no!"

"She did nothing. With Whit," he added, averting his gaze to the window. He looked, at that moment, as if he'd never smiled in his life. He was hearing himself accuse Natalie on the street in front of half a dozen bystanders of being a faithless tease.

Now it made sense. Mack had gotten drunk because he thought Natalie had gone straight from his arms to Whit's. Vivian had told him so, believing that Natalie and Whit had been alone for that hour. Whit had admitted it. And all the time . . .

"I'll go to her," Vivian said at once. "I'll apologize, on my knees if I have to!"

"Don't bother," he said, getting to his feet. "She won't let you past the porch. I told her she wasn't welcome here ever again." His fists clenched at his hips. "And several other things that were . . . over-heard," he added through his teeth. "She went to her graduation all alone." He had to stop because he was too choked to say another word. He went out without

182

looking at Vivian, and the door closed with a jerk behind him.

Vivian put her face in her hands and bawled. Out of her own selfishness, she'd destroyed two lives. Mack loved Natalie. And she knew — she *knew* — that Natalie loved Mack, had always loved him! It wasn't Natalie who'd betrayed them. It was Vivian herself. Her pride had been hurt because Whit preferred Natalie, but she'd been done a huge favor. She was besotted enough with the man to have given him all the money he'd asked for. She'd had a narrow escape, for which she had Natalie to thank. But they weren't friends anymore. They'd pushed Natalie out of their lives. It was wishful thinking to suppose she'd forgive them or ever give them a chance to hurt her again. She'd never really been loved, unless it was by the parents who'd been so tragically killed in her childhood. She was alone in the world, and she must feel it now more than ever before. Vivian took a deep breath and dried her eyes. Surely there was some way, something she could do, to make amends. She had to.

Mack went off on a prolonged business trip the next day. He barely spoke to

Vivian on his way out, and he looked like death warmed over. She could only imagine how he felt, after the way he'd behaved. Natalie might forgive him one day, but she'd probably never be able to forget.

It took her two days to get up enough courage to drive over to Natalie's house and knock on the door. She got a real shock when the door was opened, because there were two suitcases sitting on the floor, and Natalie was dressed for travel.

"Natalie, could I speak to you for a minute?" Vivian asked hesitantly.

"A minute is all I have," came the cool, distant reply. "I thought you were my cab. I have to get to the airport. One of my college professors is letting me fly with her to Dallas."

"What's in Dallas?" Vivian asked, shocked.

"My new job." Natalie looked past her at a cab that was just pulling into the driveway. She checked to make sure she had her purse and all the documents she needed before she lifted her suitcases and put them on the porch. She locked the door while Vivian stood nearby, speechless.

"I've put the house on the market," she continued. "I won't be coming back."

"Oh, Nat," Vivian whispered miserably.

"I lied. I lied to Mack. I thought . . . You were downstairs and so was Whit, for an hour or more. Whit didn't deny what I accused him of doing with you. But I didn't know Mack had come home."

Natalie looked straight at her. In that instant she looked as formidable as Vivian's taciturn brother. "Mack believed you," she said. That was all. But it was more than a statement of fact. It meant that he didn't even suspect that Natalie might be innocent. She was tarred and feathered and put on a rail without qualm.

"I'm his sister. I've never lied to him before," she added. "Nat, I have to tell you something. You have to listen!"

"Are you the lady who wants to go to the airport?" the cabdriver asked.

"Yes, I am," Natalie said, carrying her bags down the steps without another word to Vivian.

"Don't go!" Vivian cried. "Please don't go!"

"There's nothing left in Medicine Ridge for me, and we both know it, Vivian," she told the other woman without meeting her eyes as the cabdriver put both her bags in the trunk and then went to open the back door for Natalie to get into the cab. "You've finally got what you wanted.

185

Aren't you happy? I'll never be even an imagined potential rival for any of your boyfriends again."

"I didn't know," Vivian moaned. "I jumped to conclusions and hurt everybody. But please, Natalie, at least let me apologize! And don't blame Mack for it. It's not his fault."

"Mack doesn't want me," Natalie said heavily. "I suppose I knew it from the beginning, but he made it very clear the last time I saw him. He'll date Glenna and be very happy. Maybe you will, too. But I'm tired of being the scapegoat. I'm going to find a new life for myself in Dallas. Goodbye, Vivian," she said tersely, still without looking in Vivian's direction.

Vivian had never felt so terrible in all her life. She stood on the steps, alone, and watched the best friend she'd ever had leave town because of her.

"I'm sorry," she whispered to the retreating cab. "Oh, Natalie, I'm so very sorry!"

She had to tell Mack that Natalie had gone, of course. That was almost as hard as watching Natalie leave. She found him in his study, at the computer, making decisions about restocking. He looked up when he saw her at the door.

"Well?" he asked.

She went into the room and closed the door behind her. She looked washed out, miserable, defeated.

"I went to apologize to Natalie," she began.

His face tautened, and he looked a little paler. But he gathered himself together quickly and only lifted an eyebrow as he dropped his gaze to the computer screen. "I gather that it didn't go well?"

She fingered her wristwatch nervously. This was harder than she'd dreamed. "I was just in time to see her leave."

He frowned as he lifted his head. "Leave?"

She nodded. She sat in the chair beside the desk, where she'd sat and watched him the night he got drunk. She hated telling him what happened. He'd had so much responsibility in his life, so much pain. He'd never really had anyone to love, either, except for his siblings. He'd loved Natalie. Vivian had cost him the only woman who could have made him happy.

"Leave for where?" he demanded shortly.

She swallowed. "Dallas."

"Dallas, Texas? Who the hell does she know in Texas?" he persisted, still not understanding what Vivian was saying.

187

"She's got a job there," she said reluctantly. "She's . . . selling her house. She said she wouldn't be coming back."

For a few seconds, Mack didn't speak. He stared at his sister as though he hadn't understood her. Then, all at once, the life seemed to drain out of him. He stared at the dark paneling of the wall blindly while the truth hit him squarely in the gut. Natalie had left town. They'd hurt her so badly that she couldn't even stay in the same community. Probably the gossip had been hard on her, too, because Mack had made harsh accusations in front of everyone. And how did you stop gossip, when it was never spoken in public?

He sank down into his chair without a word.

"I tried to explain," she continued. "To apologize." She swallowed hard. "She wouldn't even look at me. I don't blame her. I've ruined her life because I was selfish and conceited and obsessed with jealousy. Now that I look back, I realize that it wasn't the first time I saw Nat as a rival and treated her accordingly. I've been an idiot. And I'm sorry, Mack. I really am."

His chest rose and fell. He toyed with the pencil on the desk, trying to adjust to a world without at least the occasional glimpse of Natalie. Now that he'd lost her for good, he knew how desperately he loved her. It was a hell of an irony.

"I could go to Dallas and try to make her listen," Vivian persisted, because he looked so defeated. Her brother, the steel man, was melting in front of her.

His shoulders seemed to slump a little. He shook his head. "Let her go," he said heavily. "We've done enough harm."

"But you love her!"

His eyes closed briefly and then opened. He turned to the computer and moved the mouse to reopen his file, his face drawn and remote. He didn't say another word.

After a minute of painful silence, Vivian got up and left him there. She loved her brother. It devastated her to realize how much she'd hurt him lately. And that was nothing to what she'd done to Natalie. She could never make up for what she'd cost Natalie and her brother. But she wished she had the chance to try.

Natalie, meanwhile, had settled into a small apartment near the school. She'd interviewed for the position and after a few days, she was notified that she had the job. The teaching roster had been filled for the year, but one of the teachers had come down with hepatitis and couldn't continue, so there was a vacancy. Natalie was just what they wanted for the third graders, a bilingual teacher who could understand and communicate with the Hispanic students. She was glad she'd opted for Spanish for her language sequence instead of German, which had been her first choice. It had been one of only a few good moves she'd made in her life.

She thought about Vivian's painful visit and the admission that she'd lied to Mack about Natalie and Whit. So Mack knew, but he hadn't tried to stop her. He hadn't phoned or written. Apparently she didn't even mean that much to him. He must have meant all the terrible things he'd said to her on the street, where everyone could hear him.

Part of her realized that it was for the best. He'd said that he didn't want marriage or an affair, which could only have led to more misery for both of them. It was just as well that the bond was broken abruptly. But their history went back so far that she couldn't even conceive of life without Mack. And when Vivian was herself, they'd had such wonderful times together, along with Bob and Charles. Natalie had felt as if she belonged to the

Killains, and they to her. Now she was cut adrift again, without roots or ties. She had to adjust to being alone.

At least she had a job and a place to live. She'd found work with a temporary agency for the summer so that she could save up for a few additions to her meager wardrobe for the beginning of school in August. She would survive, she promised herself. In fact, she would thrive!

But she didn't. The days turned to weeks, and although she adjusted to her new surroundings, she still felt like an outsider. When she began teaching, she was nervous and uncertain of herself, and the children knew it and took advantage of her tentative style. Her classroom was a madhouse. It wasn't until one of the other teachers, a veteran of first days on the job, came to restore order that she could manage to teach.

She was taken gently aside and taught how to handle her exuberant students. The next day was a different story. She kept order and began to learn the children's names. She learned to recognize other members of the staff, and she enjoyed her work. But at night, she lay awake remembering the feel of Mack Killain's strong arms around her, and she ached for him.

By the second week of school, she was beginning to fit in. But on the way home she passed a small basketball court and noticed two boys who looked barely high-school age pushing and shoving each other and raging at each other in language that was appalling even in a modern culture. On a whim, she went toward them.

"Okay, guys, knock it off," she said, pushing her way between them. Unfortunately she did it just as the hand of one boy went inside his denim shirt and came out with a knife. She saw a flash of metal and felt a pain in her chest so intense that it made her fall to the ground.

"You've killed her, you fool!" one of them cried.

"It was your fault! She just got in the way!"

They ran away, still arguing. She lay there, feeling a wetness on the concrete around her chest. She couldn't get air into her lungs. She heard voices. She heard traffic. She saw the blue sky turn a blinding, painful white. . . .

Mack Killain was downloading a new package of software into his computer when the phone rang. It had been a busy summer, and the unwelcome bull roundup was under way, along with getting fattened calves ready for market and pulling out herd members that were unproductive. He'd worked himself half to death trying not to think about Natalie. He still did. She haunted him, waking and sleeping.

He picked up the receiver absently on impulse, instead of letting the answering machine take over, still loading his program while he said, "Hello?"

"Mack Killain?"

"Yes?"

"This is Dr. Hayes at the Dallas Medical Center," came a voice from the other end of the line.

Mack's heart stopped. "Natalie!" he exploded with a sense of premonition.

There was a pause. "Well, yes, I am calling about a Miss Natalie Brock. Your name and number were on an accident card in her purse. I'm trying to locate a member of her family."

"What happened? Is she hurt?" Mack demanded.

"She needs immediate surgery or she's going to die," the doctor said frankly, "but I have to have written authorization for it, and she can't sign anything. She's unconscious. I have to have a member of her family."

Mack felt his heart stop. He gripped the receiver tightly. "I'm her cousin," Mack lied glibly. "I'm the only relative she has. I'll sign for her. I can be there in two hours."

"She'll be dead in two hours," came the sharp reply.

Mack closed his eyes, praying silently. "I've got a fax machine," he said. "I can write out a permission slip on my letterhead and sign it and fax it to you. Will that do?"

"Yes. But quickly, please. Here's our fax number."

Mack jotted it down. "I'll have it there in two minutes," he promised. "Don't let her die," he added in a tone as cold as ice before he hung up.

His hands shook as he stopped the loading process and pulled up his word processor instead. He typed a quick permission note, printed it out on ranch letterhead, whipped out two pens before he found one with ink, signed it, and rushed it into the fax machine. In the time he'd promised, he had it on the way.

He cut off the computer and picked up the phone, calling a charter service in a nearby city. "I want a Learjet over here in ten minutes to take me to Dallas. Don't tell me you can't do it," he added shortly. "I'll be waiting at the local airport." He gave the location and hung up.

There was no time to pack. He went barreling out of the office just as Bob and Charles came in behind a stunned Vivian.

"What's going on?" Vivian asked in concern, because Mack's face was white.

"I have no idea. But Natalie's in a Dallas hospital about to undergo emergency surgery. I had to sign for her, so if anybody calls here and asks, we're her cousins."

"Where are you going?" Bob asked.

"To Dallas, of course," Mack said impatiently, pushing past them.

"Not without us, you aren't," Charles told him bluntly. "Natalie belongs to all of us. I'm not staying here."

"Neither am I," Bob seconded.

"Where one goes, we all go," Vivian added. "I'm the one who caused all this in the first place. Natalie needs me, and I'm going. I'll make her listen to my apology when she's well."

"I don't have time to argue with you. Get in the car. I'll lock the door."

"How are we going to get there?" Vivian

asked as she herded her tall brothers outside.

"I've got a charter jet on the way."

"Flying," Bob told his sibling. "That's
cool."

"Yeah, I like flying," Charles agreed.

"Well, I don't," Vivian muttered. "But
it's quicker than driving."

She piled into the front seat with Mack
while the two boys got in back. All the way
to the airport, Mack drove like a maniac.
By the time they arrived, the three passengers had held their collective breaths long
enough to qualify as deep-sea divers.

They spilled out in the parking lot at the
small airport. The jet was already there, as
the charter service had promised, gassed
up and ready, with its door open and the
ladder down.

Mack didn't say a word until he shook
hands with the pilot and copilot and got
into the back with his sister and brothers.
Until now, he'd had the organization of
the trip to keep his mind off the danger of
the situation.

Now, with hours with nothing to do but
think during the flight, he recalled what
the surgeon had said to him — that Natalie
could die. He had no idea what had happened. He had to know. He pulled the cell

phone he always carried from his pocket and, after checking with the pilot that it was safe to use once they were in the air, he got the number of the Dallas hospital and bullied his way verbally to a resident in the emergency room. He explained who he was, asked if the fax had been received and was told that Miss Brock was in surgery. They had no report on her condition, except that there was at least one stab wound and one of her lungs had collapsed. The resident was sorry, but he had no further information. Mack told him an approximate arrival time and hung up.

"A knife wound?" Bob exclaimed. "Our Nat?"

"She's a teacher," Vivian said miserably. "Some students are very dangerous these days."

"She teaches grammar school," Mack said disgustedly. "How could a little kid stab her?"

"It might have been someone related to one of the little kids," Charles offered.

Vivian brushed back her blond hair. "It's my fault if she dies," she said quietly.

"She's not going to die," Mack said firmly. "Don't talk like that!"

She glanced at him, saw his expression and put her hand over his. "Okay. I'm sorry."

He averted his face, but he didn't shake off her hand. He was terrified. He'd never been so frightened in all his life. If he lost Natalie, there was nothing in the world to live for. It would be the end, the absolute end of everything.

Chapter 9

When Natalie regained consciousness, there was a smell of antiseptic. Her side ached. Her lung hurt. She had a tube up her nose, and it was irritating her nasal passages. She felt bruised and broken and sick. Her eyes opened slowly to a white room with people in green gowns, moving around a room that only she seemed to occupy.

She blinked hard, trying to get her eyes to focus. Obviously, she was in a recovery room. She couldn't remember how she got there.

A deep voice, raised and urgent, was demanding access to her, and a nurse was threatening to call security. It didn't do any good. He was finally gowned and masked and let in, because a riot was about to ensue in the corridor.

There was a breeze and then a familiar face with a black eye patch hovered just above her. She couldn't quite focus. Her mind was foggy.

A big, warm hand spread against her

cheek, and the one eye above her was much brighter than she remembered it. It seemed to be wet. Impossible, of course. She was simply dreaming.

"Don't you die, damn it!" he choked huskily. "Do you hear me, Natalie? Don't you dare!"

"Mr. Killain," one of the nurses was trying to intervene.

He ignored her. "Natalie, can you hear me?" he demanded. "Wake up!"

She blinked again. Her eyes barely focused. She was drifting in and out. "Mack," she whispered, and her eyes closed again.

He was raving mad. She heard him tossing orders around as if he were in charge, and she heard running feet in response. She would have smiled if she'd been able. Every woman's dream until he opened his mouth . . .

She didn't know that she'd spoken aloud, or that the smile had been visible.

Mack had one of her small hands in his with a death grip. Now that he could see her, touch her, he was breathing normally again. But she looked white, and her chest was barely moving. He was scared to death, and it displayed itself in venomous bad temper. Somebody would probably run him out any minute, maybe arrest him for causing a disturbance. But he'd have gone through an armed camp to get to her, just to see her, to make sure that she was alive. He couldn't have imagined himself like this not so long ago.

Neither could his siblings, who stood in awe of him as he broke hospital rules right and left and sent veteran health-care workers running. This was a Mack they'd never seen before. It was obvious that he was in love with the woman lying so still and quiet in the recovery room. All of them looked at each other, wondering why they hadn't realized it a long time ago.

The surgeon — presumably the one who'd spoken to him on the telephone — came into the recovery room still wearing his operating clothes. He looked like a fire-eater himself, tall and dark-eyed and taciturn.

"Killain?" he asked.

"Yes." Killain let go of Natalie's limp hand long enough to shake the surgeon's. "How is she?"

"Lost a lower lobe of her lung," he said. "There was some internal bleeding and we'll have to keep her here for a while. The danger now is complications. But she'll make it," he added confidently.

Mack felt himself relax for the first time in hours. "I want to stay with her," he said bluntly.

The doctor raised an eyebrow and chuckled. "I think that's fairly obvious to the staff," he mused. "Since you're a relative, I don't have an objection. But we would prefer to have you wait until we can get her out of recovery and into a room. Meanwhile, it would help if you'd go to the business office and fill out some papers for her. She was brought in unconscious."

Mack hesitated, but Natalie was asleep. Perhaps it wouldn't hurt to leave her, just briefly. "All right," he said finally.

The surgeon didn't dare look as relieved as he felt. He pointed Mack toward the business office, noticing that three younger people fell in step behind him. The victim apparently had plenty of family to look after her. That lightened his step as he went toward the operating theater to start the next case.

Several hours later, Natalie opened her eyes again, groggy from the anesthetic and hurting. She groaned and touched her side, which was heavily bandaged.

A big, warm hand caught hers and lifted it away. "Be careful. You'll pull out the IV," a familiar voice said tenderly. It sounded like Mack. It couldn't be, of course.

She turned her head and there he was. She managed a smile. "I thought I was dreaming," she murmured drowsily.

"The nurses don't. They think they're having a nightmare," Bob said with a wicked glance at his brother.

"I saw an orderly run right out the front door," Charles added dryly.

"Shut up," Mack said impatiently.

"He just wants to make sure you're properly looked after, Nat," Vivian said, coming close enough to brush back Natalie's hair. "You poor baby," she added softly. "We're all going to take care of you."

"That's right," Bob agreed.

"You belong to us," Charles added firmly.

Mack didn't say anything.

Too groggy to understand much of what was going on, Natalie managed another weak smile and then grimaced. But after a minute she relaxed and went back to sleep.

Vivian studied the apparatus she was hooked to. "I think this has a painkiller unit that automatically injects her every few minutes. I'm going to ask someone."

Without another word, she went into the hall.

Bob and Charles shared a speaking glance and announced that they were going after coffee, offering to bring back a cup for their big brother.

Mack just nodded. He only had eyes for Natalie. It was like coming home after a long journey. He didn't want to do anything except sit there and look at her. Even in her weak, wan condition, she was beautiful to him. His hand curled closer around hers and gripped it securely.

All the things he'd said came back to haunt him. How could he ever have doubted her? She wouldn't lie to him. Somewhere deep inside he knew that. So only one reason for his immediate assumption of her guilt was left. He'd been fighting a rearguard action against her gentle presence with the last bit of willpower he possessed. He was blind in one eye. Someday, he might lose his sight in the other, as well. He had the responsibility for his two brothers and his sister until they could stand on their own. He hadn't felt that it was fair to inflict all that on a young woman like Natalie.

But ever since the crisis had developed, his family had been united behind him and shared his concern for Natalie. They loved her, too. He knew that there would inevitably be conflicts, hopefully small ones, but he'd seen what life without her would be like, and anything was preferable. He'd do whatever he could to make her happy, to keep her safe. Of course, when she was her old self again, she was going to want to knock him over the head with a baseball bat. He was resigned to even that.

The first order of business was to get her well. He was going to take her back to Montana if he had to wrap her in sheets tied at both ends. She might not like it, but she'd have to go. She didn't have anyplace else to recuperate, and she couldn't work. At the ranch, the four of them could take turns sitting with her.

While he was considering possibilities, Vivian came back. "It automatically injects painkillers," she announced with a smile. "I spoke with the duty nurses at their station. They have computers everywhere with records and charts. . . ." She glanced at her brother with a self-conscious smile. "It fascinates me. I didn't realize nursing was so challenging, or so complicated."

"I haven't seen a lot of nurses in here," he remarked darkly.

She grinned at him. "You will when you leave," she said, tongue in cheek.

"Don't you start," he muttered.

She hugged him and sat in the chair on the other side of the bed. "Why don't you go and get something to eat? I'll sit with Nat."

He shook his head. He had her hand firmly in his and he wasn't letting go until he knew for certain that she wasn't trying to give up.

"Want some coffee?" she persisted.

"The boys went to bring some back."

"Okay. In that case, I think I'll walk down to the canteen and get a bag of potato chips and a soft drink."

"Good idea."

She smiled to herself as she went out. He hadn't spared her a glance. She could read him like a book. He was afraid that if he left, Natalie might not recover. He was going to keep her alive by sheer will, if he had to. Vivian couldn't blame him for being concerned. Natalie did look so white and thin lying there. Vivian blamed herself for Natalie's condition. If she hadn't been so horrible, none of this would have happened. She had yet to make her own apologies. But it was nice to know that Nat would be around to hear them.

She wandered down the corridor. Back in the room, Mack leaned forward to study Natalie's sleeping face. "Poor little scrap," he murmured softly, touching her cheek with a touch light enough not to disturb her. "How did I ever think I could manage without you?"

At some level, she was aware that he was speaking to her. But she was fighting the pain and the drugs, and her mind was foggy. She felt his touch, first on her cheek and then lightly brushing her mouth. He was whispering in her ear, words that sounded like the softest kind of endearments. At that point, she was sure she was dreaming. Mack never used endearments. . . .

It was late that night before she returned to something approaching consciousness. She looked around the room with surprised amusement. Vivian was asleep in the chair by the radiator. Mack was sprawled, snoring faintly, in the chair beside her bed, with her hand still gripped in his. Beside him, on the floor, Bob and Charles were asleep sharing a blanket on the cold linoleum. She could only imagine the nursing staff's frustration trying to work around them. And wasn't there some rule about the number of visitors and how long they could stay? Then she remembered the uproar Mack had caused on his arrival, and she imagined he'd broken every rule they had already.

"Mack?" she whispered. Her voice barely carried. She tried again. "Mack?"

He stirred sleepily, and his eye opened at once. He sat up, increasing his firm hold on her hand. "What is it, sweetheart?"

The endearment was disconcerting. He stood and came closer, bending over her with evident concern. "Tell me," he asked softly. "What do you want?"

She searched his face with hungry eyes. It had been weeks since she'd seen him. There was something different. . . .

"You've lost weight," she whispered.

His gaze fell to her hand in his. "So have you."

She wanted to tell him that she'd been only half alive without him, that it was the lack of him in her life that had aged her. But she couldn't say that. She'd been hurt and someone had called him. Probably her serious condition had caused Vivian to finally tell him the truth. He'd come out of guilt. Perhaps they all had.

She pulled her hand out of his and laid it across her chest. "I don't need anything," she said, averting her face. "Thank you," she added politely.

The effect of that cool, polite reply hit him hard. She was conscious again, and she'd be remembering their last meeting and what he'd said to her. He put his hands deep in his pockets and studied her for a long minute before he went to the chair and sat down. The breath he let out was audible.

She was still groggy enough that she went back to sleep at once. Mack didn't. He sat brooding, watching her, until the first rays of dawn filtered through the venetian blinds. Around him, the boys and Vivian began to stir.

Vivian got up and looked out the door, noticing the bustle of early-morning duty shifts. "Why don't you three go get us a nice hotel suite and have a bath. I'll stay here with Natalie while they get her bathed and fed. By the time you come back, she'll be ready for visitors."

Mack was reluctant. Vivian pulled him out of the chair. "You're absolutely dead on your feet, and you look fifty," she said. "You're not going to be any good to anybody until you get some rest. Have you slept at all?"

He grimaced. "She woke up in the night," he said, as if that explained it all. His face was drawn with worry and guilt. "She remembered what I said to her. It was in her eyes."

"She'll remember what I said, too," Vivian replied. "We'll get through it. She's not a person who holds grudges. It will be all right."

He hesitated. "She isn't going to want to go home with us," he realized. His face began to tauten. "But she will, if I have to put her in a sack! If she wakes up before I come back, you tell her that!"

The loud tones woke Natalie. She winced as she moved, and her chest hurt, but her eyes lifted to Mack's hard face, and they began to sparkle. She struggled to sit up. "I'm not going . . . anywhere with you, Mack Killain," she told him in as strong a tone as she could manage in her depleted condition. "I wouldn't walk to the . . . elevator with you!"

"Calm down," Vivian said firmly, easing her down on the pillows. "When you've gotten your strength back, I'll get you a frying pan and you can lay about him with it. In fact, I'll even bend over and give you a shot at me. But for now," she added softly, "you have to get well. You can only stay in the hospital until you're back on your feet. But full recuperation takes longer — and you can't stay by yourself."

Bob and Charles were awake and

crowding around the bed with their siblings.

"Right," Charles said firmly, looking so
much like his older brother that it was un-
canny. "We'll all take care of you."

"I'll hook up my game system and teach
you how to play arcade games," Bob offered.

"I'll teach you chess," Charles seconded.

"I'll teach you how to be a real pain in
the neck," Vivian added, tongue in cheek.
"I think I wrote the book on it."

Natalie wavered as her eyes went to
Mack. His gaze was steady on her face,
quiet, and he looked almost vulnerable.
Maybe it was a trick of the light.

"You could teach her how to jump to
conclusions," Vivian murmured dryly.

"I learned that from you," he shot right
back. He turned to Natalie. "I'm not
coaxing. You're coming back with us, one
way or the other, and that's the end of it."

Natalie's eyes started flashing. "You
listen here, Mack Killain!"

"No, you listen," he interrupted firmly.
"I'm going to talk to the surgeon and find
out what sort of care you need. I'll hire a
private nurse and get a hospital bed moved
in. Whatever it takes."

Natalie's small fist hit the bedcovers in

frustration. That hurt her chest, and she grimaced.

"Temper, temper," Mack said mockingly. "That won't get you anywhere."

"I am not a parcel to be picked up and carried off," she raged. "I don't belong to you!"

He lifted one eyebrow. "In one way or another," he said very quietly, "you've belonged to me since you were seventeen." He turned to Vivian. "I'll take the boys to a hotel and come back in a couple of hours. I'll phone you as soon as we're settled and you can get in touch with us if you need to."

"Okay," Vivian said with a smile. "Don't worry," she added when he hesitated at the door. "I'll take good care of her."

He still hesitated, but after a minute he shot a last, worried look at a furious Natalie and followed the boys into the hall.

"I won't go!" Natalie choked out.

Vivian went close to the bed and gently smoothed Natalie's hair from her forehead. "Yes, you will," she said gently. "Mack and I have a lot to make up to you. I was so jealous of you that I couldn't stand it. I thought I'd die if I couldn't have Whit." She shook her head sorrowfully. "You know, he even lied to me that he'd been making out with you. You were both down-stairs for almost an hour and I didn't have a clue that Mack had come home in the meantime," she added ruefully, watching Natalie blush as she recalled what she and Mack had been doing during that time. "Whit said he'd found you more receptive than I'd ever been. It was a major mis-understanding all around, and the lie I told Mack, that I'd seen you and Whit together, didn't do anything to help matters." Her worried blue eyes met Natalie's green ones. "Can you forgive me, do you think?"

Natalie let out the anger in a slow breath. "Of course," she said. "We've been friends far too long for me to hold a grudge."

Vivian bent and kissed her cheek. "I haven't been much of a friend up until this point," she said. "But I'm going to do a better job from now on. And the first matter of business is to get you a sponge bath and some breakfast."

"Mack believed you," Natalie said.

Vivian paused on her way to the door. She came back and put a gentle hand over Natalie's where it lay on her stomach over the covers. "The night I told Mack that lie, he went into the office and locked the door and drank half a bottle of Scotch whiskey. I had to get the foreman and a locksmith to open it for me. When I finally got in, he'd passed out."

Her eyes were troubled. "He never loses control like that. That was when I knew how much I'd hurt him. And after your graduation, when Bob and Charles lit into us about not being there, he went off by himself and wouldn't even talk to us for days. I know what we did hurt you, Natalie," she concluded. "But it hurt us just as badly. I'm sorry. Mack was right about Whit all along. He's going around with another rich girl, but one who likes to gamble herself, and he's got all the money he wants for the time being. I was an idiot."

"You were in love," Natalie excused her. "It doesn't exactly make people lucid."

"Doesn't it?" Vivian asked pointedly, and with a curious smile.

"Don't ask me," the other woman replied, averting her face. "I was only seventeen when I had my first and last taste of it."

"I know," Vivian said disconcertingly. She smiled gently. "It was always Mack. And I knew it, and used it to hurt you. I regret that more than anything."

"That wasn't what I meant," Natalie ground out.

Vivian didn't press the issue. She patted her hand gently. "Everything's going to be all right. Believe that, if you don't believe another word I say."

Natalie shifted to a more comfortable position. "Did all of you come down here together?" she asked.

"Yes. Your surgeon phoned and told us you were fighting for your life and that somebody had to give permission for him to operate." She grimaced. "Mack had to fax a permission slip to him as next of kin, so if anyone asks, we're your cousins." She held up a hand when Natalie started to speak. "If he hadn't, you might have died, Nat."

"I had that accident card in my purse, the one you made me fill out with Mack's name and phone number on it," Natalie recalled. "I guess they found it when I was brought in."

Vivian hesitated. "Do you remember what happened?"

"Yes. I saw two boys fighting on a basketball court. Like an idiot, I went in to stop it." She smiled wryly. "One of them had a knife, and I was just in time to catch it in my chest. Fortunately it only cost me a little bit of one lung instead of my life."

"Next time, call the police," Vivian said

firmly. "That's their job, and they do it very well."

"Next time, if there ever is one, I will." Natalie caught Vivian's hand as she moved it. "Thank you for coming all the way here. I never dreamed that any of you would — especially Mack."

"When the boys heard, the first thing they said was that you belonged to us," Vivian told her. "And you do. Whether you like it or not."

"I like it very much." Her lower lip became briefly unsteady. "I'm glad we're still friends," she managed shakily.

"Oh, Nat!" Vivian leaned down to hug her as gently as she could. "I'm sorry, I'm so sorry! I'll never, never be so selfish and horrible again, ever!"

Natalie hugged her with her good arm and sighed as the tears poured out of her, therapeutic and comforting, hot on her pale face.

Vivian drew back and found tissues for both of them to wipe their wet eyes with, and they laughed while they did it.

"Mack still has his apologies to make," Vivian added. "I think he'll welcome the opportunity. But it's going to be hard for him, so meet him halfway, would you?"

Natalie looked worried. "He looks bad."

"He should. He's been driving himself for weeks. I won't even try to tell you how hard he's been to live with."

"That isn't anything unusual," Natalie said with her first glint of humor.

"This has been much worse than usual. If you don't believe it, try looking into the hall when he comes back. You'll see medical people running for the exits in droves." She chuckled. "We just stood and gaped at him when he walked into the recovery room and started throwing orders around. The army sure lost a great leader when he was mustered out after his tour of duty. He made captain, at that."

"Did . . . Glenna come, too?" she had to ask.

"He hasn't seen Glenna since you left town," Vivian said quietly. "He doesn't talk about her, either."

Natalie didn't comment. She was sure that Mack was trying to heal a guilt complex, although he had no reason to feel guilty. He'd made a wrong assumption and accused her of something she hadn't done, but he hadn't caused her to be stabbed. That had been her own lack of foresight in stepping into a situation she wasn't trained to handle. It could have happened anywhere.

For the moment, she nodded and laid back. Vivian left her to find the nurses.

Mack came back with the boys just after lunch. He looked rested. They all did. She supposed they'd taken the opportunity to catch a little sleep in a real bed.

The boys only stayed for a few minutes, having discovered a mall near the hospital where they could look over the video games. Vivian went to the hospital cafeteria to get herself a salad for lunch. Mack sat in the chair beside the bed and looked at Natalie, who was much more animated than she had been the night before.

He reached out and caught her fingers in his, sending a wicked tingle of sensation through her, and he smiled at her gently. "You look better. How do you feel?"

"Like I've been buffaloed," she said. She was shy with him, as she'd never been. Amazing, considering their history. They knew each other so well, almost intimately, but she couldn't find anything to say to him.

He seemed to realize that. His fingers curled closer into hers and he leaned forward. "The surgeon says you can leave Friday," he told her. "I can take you back

218

on the Learjet if you're not showing any bronchial symptoms."

"The Learjet?"

"I chartered one to bring us down here. The pilot and copilot are staying at my hotel until we're ready to leave."

"That must be costing a fortune," she blurted.

He smiled cynically. "What do you think I'm worth? In addition to a very successful cattle ranch and interests in several businesses, I own shares in half a dozen stocks that skyrocketed since I bought my first shares."

She averted her eyes. "I've got an apartment here," she began.

"You *had* an apartment here."

She stared at him, confused. "What?"

"I told your landlady you weren't coming back," he said flatly. "I had your stuff packed up, carefully, and shipped to Medicine Ridge. I even had your mail collected and filled out a form for it to be forwarded on to you back home."

"You can't!" she exclaimed. "Mack, I have a job here!"

"Oh, yes, I spoke to the principal about that," he continued, maddeningly calm. "They're sorry to lose you, but considering the length of your recovery, they have to have someone come in to replace you. You can reapply if you want to come back. But you won't want to."

"Of course I'll want to come back!" she exclaimed, stunned at the changes he'd created, the havoc he'd created in her nice new life. "You can't do this!"

"I've already done it, Nat," he replied, standing to loom over her, still holding her hand. "And when you have time to think about it, you'll realize that it was the only thing I could do," he added somberly. "Leaving you here alone was never an option, not even if I'd hated you."

She dropped her eyes to his big, lean hand holding hers. It was tanned, like his face, from the long hours he spent working on the ranch. "I thought you did hate me, when I left."

He laughed with pure self-contempt. "I know you did. Viv was right, I could sure teach you how to jump to conclusions." His eye narrowed. He put a hand on the pillow beside her head and leaned close. "But there are a lot of other things I'd rather teach you."

"What things?" she asked breathlessly.

"What I promised I would, when you were seventeen." His mouth brushed her lips as gently as a breath, lingering, tasting, arousing. "Don't you remember, Natalie? I said that, when the time came, I was going to teach you how to make love."

Chapter 10

Natalie couldn't believe she'd actually heard him say that, and in a tone so tender that she hardly recognized it. It was difficult to think, anyway, with his hard mouth making little tingles of excitement everywhere it touched her face.

"Do you think I'm joking?" he asked when she didn't answer him. He bent, his breath whispering against her parted lips. "All the teasing stopped when Dr. Hayes called me and said you were at the point of death," he added tautly. His head lifted, and he looked into her eyes. "From now on, it's totally serious."

She didn't understand. Her expression told him so.

He brushed his mouth softly over her lips, careful not to take advantage of the situation or cause her even more pain. "I should never have let you leave Medicine Ridge in the first place," he said gruffly.

"You told me I wasn't welcome at the ranch ever again," she admonished, her lower lip trembling.

He actually groaned. He kissed her with something that felt like utter desperation and visibly had to force himself to stop. His hand was faintly unsteady as it pushed back her disheveled hair and traced her oval face. "I thought you went from me to him," he confessed huskily. "I couldn't bear the thought."

Her expression lightened. Her heart seemed to lift. For the first time, she reached to touch his hard mouth. "As if I could," she said with wistful sadness.

He brought her palm to his lips and kissed it hungrily. "Weeks of misery," he said heavily, "all because Vivian and I jumped to conclusions."

"It's hard to trust people. I ought to know." She searched his one beautiful eye slowly. She was uncertain with him, hesitant. The medicine was still affecting her, and she was wary of his sudden affection. She didn't trust it. Worse, she was remembering her past. There had never been a person she loved that she didn't lose. First her parents and then Carl; even if Carl hadn't been in love with her, he'd been her first real taste of it.

"Such a somber expression," he said gently. "What are you thinking?"

"That I've lost everybody I ever loved,"

she whispered involuntarily, shivering.

His head lifted and he looked straight into her wide, worried eyes. "You won't lose me," he said quietly.

Her heart ran wild. Now she was certain that she was hearing things. She opened her mouth to ask him to say it again, but just as she did, the nurse came in to check her vitals. Mack only smiled at her frustration and went in the hall to stretch his legs.

When he came back, it was as if he hadn't said anything outrageous at all. He started outlining travel plans, and by the time he finished, Vivian and the boys were back and conversation remained general.

Natalie's lungs were clear by Friday morning, and the surgeon, Dr. Hayes, released her for travel home in the Learjet. Mack lifted her out of the wheelchair at the hospital entrance and into the hired car, which they took to the airport. Less than an hour later, they were airborne, and by late afternoon, they were landing in Medicine Ridge.

The foreman had driven the Lincoln to the airport and had another ranch hand follow him in one of the ranch trucks. That made enough room for the Learjet's weary passengers to ride in the car to the ranch house. There, Mack picked Natalie up in his arms and, holding her just a little too close, he mounted the front steps and carried her over the threshold.

He glanced at her with a faintly possessive smile as he stopped just briefly in the vestibule to search her soft eyes.

"You don't have to carry me," she whispered, aware that the boys had headed straight for the kitchen and Vivian had gone ahead of them upstairs to open the guest room door for them.

"Why not?" he mused, bending to brush her mouth lazily with his. "It's good practice."

Practice for what, she wondered wearily, but she didn't question the odd remark. She moved her arm and grimaced as her whole side protested. The wound was still painful.

"Sorry," he said gently. "I keep forgetting the condition you're in. We'll go right on up."

He carried her easily up the long, graceful staircase to the guest room that adjoined his bedroom. She gave him a worried look.

"I'm not having you at the other end of the house in this condition," he told her as he passed Vivian and went into the airy room with its canopied double bed, where he gently put her down. "I'm going to leave the connecting door open, as well. If you need me in the night, all you have to do is call me. I'm a light sleeper." He glanced at his sister with a speaking glance. "Something I can't say for anybody else in this family."

Vivian grimaced. "I do eventually wake up," she said defensively.

"I've got your pain medication in my pocket," he added. "If you need it at bedtime, I'll make sure you get it. Vivian can help you into a gown."

"Something nice and modest," Vivian murmured, tongue in cheek, with a wicked glance at her brother.

"Good idea," he said imperturbably. He paused at the door and that good eye twinkled. "And I'll wear pajamas for a change."

Vivian chuckled at Natalie's flushed cheeks as Mack left them alone. "You're in no condition for any hankypanky," she reminded her friend. "So stop worrying and just concentrate on getting well. You'll never convince me that you won't feel safer with Mack a few yards away in the night."

"I will," Natalie had to admit. "But I still feel like I'm imposing."

"Family doesn't impose," her friend shot right back. "Now let's get you into something light and comfortable, and then I'll go and see what's on the menu for supper. I don't know about you, but I'm starved!"

It came as a surprise when Mack brought a tray to her room and sat down to have his supper with her. But other surprises followed. Instead of going to work in the study, as was his habit, he read her a selection of first-person accounts of life in Montana before the turn of the century. History was her favorite subject, and she loved it. She closed her eyes and listened to his deep voice until she fell asleep.

She'd been heavily sedated in the hospital and she hadn't had nightmares. But her first night in a comfortable bed, she relived the stabbing. She was lifted close to a warm, comforting chest and held very gently while soothing endearments were whispered into her ear. At first it felt like a dream. But the heat and muscle of the chest felt very real, like the thick hair that covered it. Her hand moved experimentally in the darkness.

"Mack?" she whispered hesitantly.

"I hope you don't expect to wake up and find any other man in your bed from now on," he murmured sleepily. His big hand smoothed her hair gently. "You had a nightmare, sweetheart. Just a nightmare. Try to go back to sleep."

She blinked and lifted her face just enough to look around. It was her bedroom, but Mack was under the covers with her and had apparently been there for some time.

He pulled her down and held her as close as he dared. "Did you really think I meant to leave you alone in here after what you've been through?" he asked somberly.

"But what will the family think?" she asked worriedly.

"That I love you, probably."

She was so drowsy that she couldn't make sense of the words. "Oh."

"Which is why we're getting married, as soon as you're back on your feet."

She wondered if painkillers could make people hallucinate. "Now I know I'm still asleep," she murmured to herself.

"No such luck. Try to sleep before I do something stupid. And for the record, my sister's idea of a modest nightgown is sick. Really sick. I can feel your skin through that damned thing!"

He probably could. She could certainly feel his chest against her breasts much better than she was comfortable doing. But she still wasn't quite awake. Her fingers curved into the thicket of hair that covered his breastbone. "What sort of stupid thing were you thinking of trying?" she asked conversationally.

"This." His hand found the tiny buttons that held the bodice together and efficiently slipped them so that she was lying skin to skin against his chest.

She felt her nipples go hard at once, and she gasped with the heated rush of sensation that made her heart race.

"That's exactly how I feel," he murmured dryly, "a few inches lower."

It took her a few seconds to realize what he was saying, and she was glad that the darkness hid her face. "You pig!" she exclaimed.

He chuckled. "I can't resist it. You do rise to the bait like a trophy fish," he commented. "You'll get used to it. I've been blinder than I look, but a lot of things became clear when that surgeon phoned me. The main one was that you belong to me. I'm not a perfect physical specimen, and I've cornered the market on dependents, but you could do worse."

"There's nothing wrong with you," she said quietly. "You have a slight disability."

"We both know I could go blind eventually, Natalie," he said, speaking to her as he never had before. "But I think we could cope with that, if we had to."

"Of course we could," she replied.

His hand smoothed her hair. "The boys and Vivian love you, and you love them. We may have disagreements, but we'll be a family, just the same. A big family, if we all have children," he added, chuckling. "But children will be a bonus."

Her hand flattened on his chest. "I'd like to have a child with you," she said daringly. She felt his heart jump when she said it. "Would you like a son or a daughter?" she added.

"I'd like anything we get," he said quietly. "And so would you."

That sounded permanent. She smiled and couldn't stop smiling. Children meant a commitment.

"Yes. So would I," she said, closing her eyes with a long, heartfelt sigh of contentment.

His hand tensed on her hair. "I wouldn't do too much of that," he cautioned.

"What?"

"I can feel every cell of your body from the waist up, Nat," he said in a strained tone. "And I've gone hungry for a while.

You aren't up to a passionate night. Not yet."

"That last bit sounds promising," she murmured.

"I'll make you a promise," he replied. "When you're in a condition to appreciate it, I'll make you glad you waited for me."

"I already am, Mack," she whispered. "I love you more than the air I breathe."

For a few seconds, he didn't say anything. Then he turned, and his mouth found hers in the darkness in a kiss that was hard and hungry and passionate but so tender that it touched her heart. But after a few seconds, when one of his legs slid against hers almost involuntarily, he stiffened and abruptly rolled over onto his back beside her, groaning as he laughed.

"I knew this was a bad idea," he sighed.

Her body was tingling with delicious sensations. She pulled herself into a sitting position, grimacing with discomfort. "Well, there goes that brilliant idea," she murmured, holding her rib cage as she eased back down.

"What brilliant idea?" he asked.

"I was going to see if I could —" She stopped dead when she realized what she was about to say. "I mean, I . . ."

There was a highly amused sound from

beside her. "If you got on top, Nat, I'd still have to hold you there, and after the first few seconds, I wouldn't be gentle. We'd reopen that wound and the pain would be vicious."

She swallowed. "Just a thought. Forget I mentioned it."

He laughed tenderly, bending to kiss her briefly. "I'll try," he said softly. "Thanks for the thought, anyway. But this isn't the time or the place. First we get married," he continued. "And then we can make all sorts of discoveries about each other."

Her heart was still racing. "It's exciting to think about that."

"For both of us," he admitted. "But we'd better quit right now, while we're ahead." He bent and brushed his mouth softly over a hard nipple, lingering to taste it with his tongue.

She caught her breath and he lifted his head to look at her in the soft glow of the small night-light.

"I like that," she whispered.

"Me, too." He was hesitating. This was a bad idea. One of the worst he'd ever had. But he was bending to her body while he was thinking it. His mouth covered her breast again, very gently, and one lean hand smoothed down her body to ease her gown up. He traced her upper thigh with slow, expert movements, making lazy and exciting forays inside it under the gown.

She started trembling. Her hands hesitated on his shoulders while she let her mind go blank except for the pleasure he was giving her. It had been so long. While she was thinking it, she said it.

"So long," he breathed urgently. "Yes, Nat. Too long!"

Her hands went between them to his broad chest and caressed him with delight, enjoying the thickness of hair and the warm muscles under it.

She felt his body tense and his hand move to a much more intimate exploration. She tried to catch his wrist, but it was too sweet to deny. She gave in, moaning as she felt the most exquisite sensations pulse through her.

She was drowning in pleasure. It was so intense that she barely felt him take her hand and guide it down his body. He'd unsnapped his pajamas and she was inside them, discovering the major difference between men and women with a fascination that was going to make her die of embarrassment sooner or later. For the moment, though, it was exciting to touch him that way. She couldn't have dreamed of doing that with anyone else.

He shifted restlessly, enticing her slow tracing to grow in confidence as he groaned aloud at her breast.

"It won't hurt you, will it?" she whispered shakily.

"What you're doing?" He shivered and his mouth grew hungry at her breast, making her moan, as well. "I'm in agony. No, don't stop!" he said quickly, catching her hand before it withdrew. "Don't stop, baby," he whispered, moving to cover her mouth with his. "I love feeling you touch me! I love it!"

She opened her lips to speak, and he invaded them as his hand moved into a more intimate exploration, one that caused her whole body to spin off into a realm she'd never known existed.

She was moving in a helpless rhythm, helping him, enticing him to continue. Her eyes opened and his was there, seeing her pleasure, watching.

"This is how it feels when a man and a woman go all the way," he whispered huskily, and before she could question the blunt statement, his touch became urgent and invasive, and she seemed to explode into a thousand pulsating, white-hot fragments under his fascinated scrutiny.

She clutched his shoulders, shivering in the aftermath, her open mouth against his bare shoulder. Seconds later, she was crying. Her chest hurt again, but her whole body felt as if it had been caressed to heaven.

"Mack," she whimpered. "Oh, Mack!"

He was kissing her, soft, undemanding caresses all over her face and throat, down to her still taut breasts and back up again. She could feel his body against her without a stitch of clothing in the way. And only then did she realize that her gown was lying on the floor somewhere.

She didn't remember the clothes being removed. She only remembered the throbbing pleasure that even in memory made her tremble.

"When we have each other, we're going to set fires," he whispered into her ear.

"I want to," she breathed into his lips. Her hands smoothed his cheeks as she looked at him with caressing eyes. "I want to right now." Her hips moved against his, feeling the hard thrust of him that he made no effort to hide.

"So do I. More than you realize," he replied tersely. "But we're not going one step further than this until you're completely healed and we're married."

"Mack!" she groaned.

"You can't take my weight," he said. "Even if you lie over me, it would be more violent than this when I went into you. And once I started, I'd lose control."

Her gasp was audible. Word pictures formed in her mind and made her flush in the dim light.

"You're still a virgin," he continued huskily. "No matter how much I arouse you, it's probably going to be uncomfortable. But I want you to know what it's going to feel like when you adjust to me. I don't want you afraid of me on our wedding night."

"As if I could be . . . after that," she whispered, pushing her face into his throat. "Oh, it was . . . glorious!"

"Watching you was glorious," he said roughly. "But we have to stop. I won't take my pleasure at the expense of your pain."

He got up abruptly, pausing to help her into her gown before he picked up his pajama trousers. He turned toward her deliberately, watching her avert her eyes.

"Are you afraid to look at me?" he asked gently.

She grimaced. "I'm sorry. It's . . . difficult."

He laughed, but it wasn't mocking

laughter. "All right, chicken." She heard his pajama trousers snap, unusually loud in the room, before he climbed into bed beside her and drew her demurely to his side.

"You're going to stay with me all night?" she whispered breathlessly.

"All night, every night, if I have to put a chastity belt on you to protect you until we're married," he said wickedly. "And I may. I want you excessively."

She nuzzled her face against his shoulder. "I felt like that, too. I didn't expect to. I've never known what it was to want someone until you started making passes at me."

"I couldn't help it," he sighed. "I'd reached the end of my patience."

"What do you mean?"

He kissed the tip of her nose. "Later. I've got work to do tomorrow. We both have to get some sleep. Okay?"

She sighed, as close to heaven as she'd ever dreamed of being. "Okay, Mack."

She let her sated body relax and curled into him, closing her eyes. He gathered her as close as he dared and pulled the covers up.

"And don't brood over what I just did to you," he murmured firmly. "It's part of the courtship ritual. We'll restrain ourselves until it's legal. In the meantime, you and Vivian can plan the wedding."

She moved drowsily. "Are you really serious?"

"Deadly," he said, and he wasn't laughing. "I wanted you when you were seventeen and I want you now. Somewhere in the middle, I fell in love without realizing it. These past few weeks have been the purest hell I've ever known. I don't want to go through them again."

"Neither do I." She touched his face in the darkness. "I'll be the best wife in the world, I promise I will. I'll take care of you until we die."

He swallowed hard. "I'll take care of you, too, Natalie," he whispered. "And I'll never stop loving you. Not even when they lay me down in the dark."

She pressed her mouth against his bare shoulder and her hands clung to him. "Not without me, you don't. Where you go, I go. No matter where."

He couldn't manage another word. He kissed her forehead with breathless tenderness and wrapped her close in the darkness.

The wedding took a lot of planning. It had to be small, because Natalie didn't recover as fast as she'd hoped to. But it had to be big enough to accommodate every-one who wanted to see them married, and that meant having it at church. They set-tled on the local Presbyterian church, and Natalie decided to have a traditional white wedding gown and to let Vivian be maid of honor. Mack decided to have two best men so that both his brothers could stand up with them. It was unconventional, but very much a family affair.

With Mack in a dark suit and Natalie in her elegant puffy-sleeved white silk dress with a long veil and a bouquet of white roses, they were married. They exchanged rings and when Mack lifted the veil to look at her for the first time as his wife, tears rained down her face as he bent and kissed her more tenderly than he ever had before. They looked at each other with expressions that brought tears to the eyes of some of the matrons in the congregation. Afterward, there was the mad dash out the door — done leisurely to accommodate Natalie's still slow pace — and the rice and ribbons. It was traditional in that respect, at least, and in the reception in the fellowship hall with the cakes and punch.

"You made the most beautiful bride in the world, Nat," Vivian said as she kissed her warmly after the ceremony. "I'm so glad things worked out, in spite of me."

Natalie laughed warmly. "We both have a lot to learn about life. Besides," she added, "every bad experience has a silver lining. Look at what mine has produced. And not only for me," she added wryly.

Vivian wrinkled her nose as she smiled. "Imagine me, in nursing school," she chuckled. "But the nurses in Dallas said I was a natural, and I think I am. I love the work, the equipment, everything. I daresay if I study hard, I'll make a decent nurse."

"You could make a decent doctor, if you wanted to," Mack added as he joined them to slip a possessive arm around his new wife. "We can afford medical school."

"I know that," Vivian said. "But I'm not really keen on spending ten years in school, just the same. Besides," she said with a grin, "everyone knows that the nurses are the real power in hospitals!"

Natalie laughed. "You certainly would be."

Mack kissed his sister's cheek. "You've changed a lot in the past few months," he pointed out. "I'm very proud of you."

Vivian flushed with pleasure. "I'm proud of you, too, big brother. Even though it took you so long to realize that marriage isn't a trap."

He searched her face quietly. "I was afraid that it might be too much responsibility for Natalie to take on. But uncertainty is part of life. Families band together and get through the bad times."

"Indeed they do," Vivian seconded. "I'm so glad we all had a second chance. Look what wonderful things we've done with it!"

"And the most wonderful is only a few hours away," Mack whispered in Natalie's ear a few minutes later as they were preparing to leave on their brief honeymoon to Cancún.

Natalie pressed her hand against his cheek and felt him lift and turn it to press his lips to the palm. "I've waited a long time for you," she said cheekily. "You said you'd be worth it."

He chuckled. "Wait and see."

They had Vivian and the boys drive them to the Medicine Ridge airport, where they took the Learjet to Cancún. They were booked into a luxury hotel on the long island just off the mainland, with one of the most beautiful sugary white beaches in the world. It looked like paradise to Natalie.

"It's so beautiful," she kept repeating after they'd checked in and were standing on their private balcony. "It looks like a picture postcard!"

"You can't swim just yet," he reminded her. "But would you like to go and walk on the beach?"

She turned to him and smiled softly. "Would you?"

He pursed his lips and gave her lithe body in the peach silk dress a long and ardent scrutiny. "I think we both know what *I'd* like to do," he mused. "But I'll humor you."

"It would be nice to look for shells," she said. "And besides, it's not dark yet."

He blinked. "I beg your pardon?"

"It's not dark. I mean, it's broad daylight." She hesitated, because he wasn't getting it at all. She flushed a little. "I couldn't possibly take off my clothes in the light and do . . . that . . . in bed with you looking at me!"

Chapter 11

He stared at her with utter astonishment. "My God!"

He looked as if she'd thrown a pie in his face. She put her hands on her hips. "My God, what?" she demanded. He sure was acting funny.

He took the tourist booklet out of her hands and put it on the round table inside the sliding door. He pulled her to him, very gently, and bent to her mouth.

It was the first time he'd kissed her with intent, as a lover instead of a fiancé. Despite their intimacy her first night back at the Killain house, she hadn't dreamed there were such deep levels of intimacy in a simple kiss, until she felt her knees buckle and her body begin to burn with sensations she'd never felt.

She held onto his arms as his big, warm hands began a slow, teasing exploration of her figure that rose to just under her breasts, and around them, without touching them at all. After a few seconds, her body began to follow them, to entice them and finally to plead for the teasing touch that he denied her. When it came, when she felt his hands close around them, she moaned harshly and caught his wrists to hold his hands there.

It was like that night he'd touched her so intimately and taught her the sensations her untried body could feel with him. He'd taken her to heights that she'd dreamed about and moaned hungrily over in the time before the wedding. He hadn't come very close to her in the meantime, apparently dead serious about abstaining until the rings were in place. He had continued to share her bed, but with the hall door cracked open and a resistance to all her flirting that made her reel. He was affectionate, gentle, even tender — but there was nothing indiscreet or urgent. Until now.

She never felt him ease her down on the bed. Each caress was followed by one that was more enticing, more teasing, more provocative. Her world narrowed to the needs of her body. She'd gone hungry for him in recent days. She ached to have him against her. She wanted his hands on her bare skin. She wanted his eyes on her. She wanted utter, absolute possession. She arched her back and ground her mouth into his, her hands trembling as they locked behind his head and guided those expert lips to her breasts. They were bare, although she didn't realize it until his mouth fastened hard onto a taut nipple and began to suckle it. She made a sound that she didn't recognize and twisted up to prolong the sweet agony of the contact. It had been so long. Too long. Ages too long!

In the tense, lazy minutes that followed, she was all too eager to shed her clothing, because her body was hungry for his mouth and his hands. They felt warm in the faint chill of the air conditioner, but she was blind to the light that flowed in through the venetian blinds as he ripped the cover off the bed and pushed the pillows after it. His body moved lazily against hers between urgent unfastening and unbuttoning. He managed to get the fabric out of the way and follow it with two pairs of shoes in a blind, throbbing heat that had both of them out of their minds with desire.

"I thought I'd go mad before the ceremony," he said against her breasts. "I ached like a boy before his first time. All I could think about was that night we lay naked together in your bed, and you let me satisfy you!"

"I thought about it, too," she groaned,

clinging to him. "I want it again. I want you!"

"I want you, too," he said huskily, suckling her a little roughly in his ardor. "More than you realize!"

He lifted away from her for a minute, his expression barely controlled, tense. He looked at her nudity with raging desire while he gauged her readiness for what was to come. He traced a torturous path down her taut body and touched her blatantly, his eye narrow and glittery.

"Yes, you're ready," he breathed.

She wondered how he knew, but before she could ask, he was moving her closer to him with an expertise she couldn't begin to match.

He rolled onto his side, pulling her between his long, powerful legs. His hands settled on her slender hips, moving her against the hard thrust of him in an arousing rhythm as he played hungrily with her soft, parted lips.

One of his long legs eased between both of hers in a teasing motion that was even more arousing than the play of his warm hands on her bare skin. She shivered and tried to get closer.

"Don't rush it," he said tenderly. "I have to be slow, so that I don't hurt you too much. Let me show you what I want you to do."

He guided her with his hips until she was right up against him in an intimacy they'd never shared unclothed. Her eyes widened as she felt him in the most intimate place of all. She jerked a little at the unfamiliar closeness.

"That's it, sweetheart," he coaxed, both hands on her hips, drawing her over him tenderly so that he moved slowly against the faint barrier she could feel.

Her hands bit into his hard arms. She stared at him, fascinated at the play of expressions on his taut features as his body began to invade hers with the advent of a sharp, unexpected pain. He hesitated, and his hand went between them, working magic on her tense muscles.

She began to shiver with the onrush of pleasure, diverted from the pain. He was so blatant with his ardor that she lost the last vestiges of fear and began to move with him, hungry, greedy for more of the fierce pleasure he was teaching her.

"It won't hurt for long," he promised as he began to move closer. "I'll be careful with you."

"I don't care," she choked, pushing against him in an agony of need. Her eyes closed on a sob. "Oh, please, Mack! It aches so!"

"Natalie," he groaned, losing his patience in the heated brushing of her thighs against his. He brought her against him hard while his mouth ground into hers. He felt her body open to him completely, hesitate, flinch briefly.

His eye opened and looked into both of hers, but she wasn't hesitating, she wasn't protesting. Her eyes were blind with passion, her face flushed with desire.

His hands contracted while he watched her face. She gasped at the slow, deep, sweet invasion and moaned sharply as her body adjusted to this new and wonderful intimacy.

"Don't tense," he whispered.

"I'm not!" she whispered back, swallowing hard. "It feels . . ." Her eyes closed and she gasped. "So good, Mack! So . . . good! So good!"

She was sobbing with every fierce movement of his hips, her hands clutching at him, her body following the quick, hard dance of his in the silence of the room. Spirals of pleasure were running through her like flames, lifting her, turning her against him. She felt him inside her and the pleasure began to pulse, like the quick,

248

sharp beat of her heart as he moved in a deep, throbbing rhythm. She had a glimpse of his face going taut, and she heard his breath become torturous as the movement increased in fury and insistence.

She was reaching for some incredibly sweet peak of pleasure. It was there, it was . . . there. If only she could find the right position, the right movement, the right . . . yes! She lifted to him in an arch, gasping.

"There?" he whispered. "All right. Here we go. Don't fight it . . . don't fight it . . . don't . . . Natalie!"

His voice throbbed like her body, like the pulse that was beating in her eyes, her brain, her body, a heat that was as close to pain as it was to pleasure. And all at once, it became an unbearably wonderful tension that pulled and pulled and suddenly snapped, throwing her against him in an agony of pleasure. She shivered and felt him shiver as they clung together in the most delicious ecstasy she'd ever experienced in her life.

She heard his voice at her ear, harsh and deep, as his body clenched one last time and finally relaxed, pressing her into the mattress with the weight of him. Her arms curled around his long back and her eyes closed and she smiled, achingly content as she held him like that, heavy and damp and warm, vulnerable in his satiation, on her heart.

All too soon, he leaned up, his gaze holding on her rapt face. He smiled gently. "Well?"

She knew what he was asking. She smiled shyly and hid her face in his warm, damp throat.

He rolled over, still joined to her, holding her close. "How's the rib cage?"

"It's fine," she whispered.

"And what do you think about love-making, Mrs. Killain?" he whispered wickedly.

"I think it's wonderful," she blurted. "I never would have believed it could be so sweet. And I was afraid!" she added, laughing.

"I noticed." He kissed her nose. "Are you ready for a shock?"

She looked at him, puzzled. "A shock?"

"Uh-huh."

While she was trying to work it out, he lifted her away from him, and she looked down. Her face went scarlet.

"Now you know, don't you?" he asked with a worldly wisdom she couldn't match. He put her down and got out of bed, magnificently naked and not a bit inhibited. He went to the small icebox and pulled out a bottle of beer, which he took to bed, sprawling on top of the sheets against the headboard.

"Come on," he coaxed, opening his arm to gather her beside him. "You'll get used to it. Marriage is an adventure. You have to expect startling discoveries."

"This is one," she murmured, still shy of him like this.

He chuckled. "I'm just flesh and blood. The mystery will get less mysterious as we go along. We're through the worst of the honeymoon shocks, though."

"Think so?" she mused. "You haven't seen me with my hair in curlers and no makeup yet."

He bent and kissed the tip of her nose. "You're beautiful to me. It won't matter what you wear. Or how you look. I love you. Now more than ever."

He opened the beer and took a sip, putting the bottle to her lips. She made a face.

"It isn't good beer," he agreed. "But it's cold and good for the sort of thirst we've worked up." He took another sip and let his eyes run down the length of her soft body, lingering on the places he'd touched and kissed until she flushed. "You really are a knockout," he murmured. "I knew you were nicely shaped, Mrs. Killain, but you're more than I ever expected."

"That goes for me, too," she said.

He kissed her lips tenderly. "Feel like doing that again?" he whispered. "Or is it going to be uncomfortable?"

She rolled onto her side and slid one of her legs to the inside of his. "It won't be uncomfortable," she whispered. She rubbed her body against him and felt him tense with a sense of pride and accomplishment. "I want you."

The beer bottle barely made it to the table without overturning as he pulled her to him and kissed her with renewed passion. He really shouldn't have been capable of this much desire this soon, but he wasn't going to question a nice miracle. His mouth opened on her eager one, and he forgot the rest of his questions.

That evening, they sat on the balcony after a light supper, drinking cola and watching the moon rise over the Gulf of Mexico. They sat side by side, holding hands and glancing at each other every few seconds to make sure that it was all real.

"In all my dreams, it was never like this," she confessed softly.

"Not in mine, either," he replied gently.

"I don't like to leave you even long enough to take a shower." His gaze went hungrily to her face. "I never thought it could be like this, Natalie," he breathed. "Not so that I feel as if we're sewn together by invisible threads."

She drew the back of his big hand to her lips. "This is what they say marriage should be," she said dreamily. "But it's more than I hoped for."

His fingers curled into hers. "I know." He glanced at her hungrily. "You'll never know how I felt when Vivian confessed that she'd lied. I couldn't bear the thought that I'd almost lost you."

"It's all in the past," she said tenderly. "Speaking of your sister, Vivian phoned while you were showering," she said suddenly. "She said that Bob and Charles have gone hunting with that Marlowe man and she was going to spend the weekend cramming for her first test."

"I told the boys not to go off and leave her alone," he said grimly.

"Stop that," she chided. "Vivian's grown, and the boys practically are. You have to stop dictating every move they make."

He glared at her. "Wait until we have kids that age, and tell me that then!" he chided.

She sighed over him, her eyes full of wonderful dreams. "I'd like one of each," she mused. "A boy to look like you, and a girl who'll spend time with me when I'm working in the kitchen or the garden, or who'll be old enough for school when I go back to teaching."

"Planning to?" he asked comfortably.

"Not until the children are old enough to go, too," she said. "We can afford for me to stay home with them while they're small, and I will. When they're old enough to go to school, I'll go back to work."

He brought her hand to his mouth and smiled. "Sensible," he agreed. "And I'll change diapers and give bottles and teach them how to ride."

She studied his handsome face and thought back over all the long years they'd known each other, and the trials they'd faced together. "It's the bad times that bring us close," she commented softly.

"Yes," he said. "Like fire tempering steel. We've seen the best and worst of each other, and we have enough in common that even if we didn't have the best sex on two continents, we'd still make a good marriage."

She pursed her lips. "As it is," she said, "we'll make an extraordinary one."

"I couldn't agree more." He lifted his can of soda and she lifted hers, and they made a toast.

Out on the bay, a cruise ship was just coming into port, its lights making a fiesta of the darkness, a jeweled portrait in the night. Natalie felt like that inside, like a holiday ship making its way to a safe harbor. The orphan finally had a home where she belonged. She clasped her husband's hand tight in her own and sighed with pure joy.

About the Author

Diana Palmer is a prolific writer who got her start as a newspaper reporter. As one of the top ten romance writers in America, she has a gift for telling the most sensual tales with charm and humor. Diana lives with her family in Cornelia, Georgia.